MURDER IN THE
BRITISH QUARTER

A QING DYNASTY MYSTERY BOOK 2

AMANDA ROBERTS

Murder in the British Quarter

A Qing Dynasty Mystery

Murder
IN THE
British Quarter

Amanda Roberts

Red Empress Publishing
www.RedEmpressPublishing.com

Copyright © Amanda Roberts
www.TwoAmericansinChina.com

Cover by Cherith Vaughan
www.EmpressAuthorSolutions.com

ALSO BY AMANDA ROBERTS

Fiction

Threads of Silk

The Qing Dynasty Mysteries

Murder in the Forbidden City

Murder in the British Quarter

The Touching Time Series

The Emperor's Seal

The Empress's Dagger

The Slave's Necklace

Nonfiction

The Crazy Dumplings Cookbook

Crazy Dumplings II: Even Dumplinger

The riot had started in the dark hours of the morning, when the Chinese employees of the Foreign Legation had begun venturing into the Chinese portions of Peking to run their morning errands. They took the news of the murder with them, spreading truth mixed with hearsay and rumor and stirring up dissent. By the time Prince Kung and Inspector Gong arrived, the gates had been closed and hundreds of angry people had gathered outside the legation.

"Can you believe this?" Prince Kung asked. "All over some peasant girl. If she'd been killed anywhere else in China, no one would have given a shit about her."

Inspector Gong grunted his agreement as he peeked out the windows of the sedan chair. He rarely ever traveled in such a stately manner, but he had first been summoned to Prince Kung's mansion, and together they traveled to the legation. When it came to troubles between the foreigners and Chinese, Prince Kung was the man people turned to. Prince Kung had filled Inspector Gong in on what little he knew about the situation on the way there.

A serving girl had been murdered in the home of a wealthy British merchant overnight in the British Quarter of the legation. They had sent for the British police, but of course the other Chinese servants knew what was happening. Word about the murder spread, and people were, rightly, concerned that the murder would just be covered up. If she had been killed by a foreigner, the killer would never see justice. If people hadn't rioted, the situation may have completely gone unnoticed by the Chinese authorities, not that they could do much about it.

The chair bearers stopped outside the crowd of people. Even though the front gate was still many meters away, they could get no closer. Prince Kung and Inspector Gong climbed out of the chair. The prince motioned for his guards to clear the people out of his way. Fortunately, Prince Kung was popular with the people, so few put up a fight as the prince and the inspector made their way through the crowd. In front of the gate, there was an opening in the sea of people. On the ground, two elderly people were knocking their foreheads to the ground and wailing, a traditional way of publicly mourning when someone had been wronged.

"You are the girl's parents," Inspector Gong said loudly over the din of people.

The man stopped and looked up at him while the woman continued her lament. "We are," he said. "Our girl, our beautiful girl, was ripped from us this night. Where are lowly ones such as ourselves to find comfort, much less justice? These white devils kill us and we are supposed to do nothing?"

At that, the crowd erupted again and pushed in toward the prince and the inspector. The prince's guards held the people back, but worry showed on his face.

"I'll need to question her parents further," the inspector said softly in the prince's ear.

The prince nodded. "But not here, not now. That man knows what he is doing. He's whipping up the crowd."

Inspector Gong nodded. The father wasn't just mourning, he was encouraging the rioters. To what end, the inspector wasn't sure yet. He would have to parse that out later.

The prince led the inspector to the gate, which was lined with a dozen very nervous British guards. The head guard held his hand up as they approached.

The guard said something in English that Inspector Gong didn't understand, but his meaning was clear. He wasn't going to let them in.

The prince grew indignant and yelled, in English, at the guard, who looked sufficiently shaken when the prince was done. The guard quickly saluted and then bowed in apparent confusion about how to react to the prince, especially in such a situation. He stammered something else and then nearly ran to the guard room on one side of the gate and opened a small window in the back to talk to someone on the other side.

He returned quickly and said something, accompanied with a bow. He indicated that the prince should follow him. The guard led them to a small door inside the large gate and ushered the prince, Inspector Gong, and the prince's guards through.

They were welcomed by several foreign men in various dress, some in uniforms, some simply in suits. Inspector Gong knew nothing about foreigners or their ways, so he had no way of knowing who the men were, so he simply followed the prince's lead. He shook hands and nodded his head, but he didn't speak. Even though he could say hello, thank you, and other small words, he had no confidence in his English ability and knew he would speak heavily accented. He didn't want to give any appearance of weakness in front of people who he might have to, somehow, question about the girl's murder.

Prince Kung, on the other hand, was fluent in English. As he spoke to the men, he nodded his head gravely and then forcefully explained the situation. They argued back and forth for a moment, then the foreigners turned away.

The prince explained more of the situation to Inspector Gong as they followed the foreigners. "These men are the chief of police for the British citizens, the British ambassador, and the British, American, and German consuls. They want to handle the situation internally, of course, but I told them that the situation had escalated beyond that now. If they want to avoid an international incident, we have to be allowed to conduct our own investigation or at least be part of their investigation. The locals need to be reassured that justice will be done."

Inspector Gong nodded his head.

As they walked, Inspector Gong took in the sites. He had never been into the Foreign Legation before. Like the Forbidden City, whose southern wall loomed just to the north of the legation, the Foreign Legation was a world apart. Only foreigners were allowed to live here, except for the Chinese servants they often employed, and the different sections of the legation took on the aspects of the country they represented. The finest dress shops could be found in the French Quarter, the best food could be found in the German Quarter, and the most opulent houses could be found in the British Quarter.

The inspector was nearly awed by the large houses that loomed two and three stories tall like white teeth ready to gnash anyone unwelcome who walked by. The houses had green lawns and wrought iron fences. White faces peeked out of the windows on the upper floors as they walked past. The inspector chuckled to himself. Nosey neighbors were universal, it seemed.

They finally arrived at what appeared to be the largest and most well-appointed house in the British Quarter. A crowd had gathered outside, both of uniformed officers and average lookyloos, both foreign and Chinese.

Inspector Gong examined the house. A window on the third floor was shattered and the glass had fallen on the walkway leading up to the front door and was being trampled by people standing around unhelpfully. He looked across the street and saw that there were several houses of the same height.

The prince and the inspector were led inside the house. Inspector Gong had been in some fancy homes in his life, even the Forbidden City, but Chinese decor was damn near austere compared to this. It was downright garish. The floors and walls were a dark mahogany wood and a large staircase greeted them. The inspector looked up and saw a crystal chandelier. There were gilded mirrors and picture frames on every wall. Elaborate carpets covered the floors. Every table top, of which there were many, were covered with lace and countless knickknacks. He was surprised to see several Chinese items among the mess—ink and wash paintings on the walls, embroidered lotus slippers on a table, and a Tang Dynasty terracotta horse standing in one corner.

They were taken to the first room in the left, which had similar decorations but also had plush green couches and chairs for sitting. A tall portly man with thick, fair facial hair was standing there, drinking something out of a small crystal goblet. A woman with similarly round features and the largest, most prominent bosom Inspector Gong had ever seen was sitting on the couch, a handkerchief to her face.

"This is the owner of the house, and the employer of the young woman," the prince explained as he shook hand with the man. "His name is Mr. John Gibson."

Inspector Gong nodded and shook the man's hand, but remained silent.

The prince and Mr. Gibson talked back and forth for a few minutes, of which the inspector understood nothing. He looked at the woman for a moment. At first he thought she had been crying, but then he realized she wasn't. She was holding the handkerchief to her face, but her eyes were not red or puffy and her cheeks were dry. She did have a bit of a far off look to her, as if she was lost in thought, but she seemed more worried, possibly angry. He then noticed her foot was tapping anxiously. Of course, it was natural to be apprehensive if someone was murdered in your home, but the inspector had a feeling there was some other cause for her unease. He hoped he would have a chance to chat with her at some point, but he doubted it.

"No! Certainly not," Mr. Gibson said heatedly, using some of the few words the inspector understood.

The prince, though, did not give up and continued to press his case. Finally, Mr. Gibson stomped toward the stairway and led them upstairs.

"He doesn't want us investigating," the prince explained.

"Naturally," Inspector Gong replied.

"I'm doing my best here. He is allowing us to see the body and the crime scene, but not for long."

Inspector Gong nodded and followed Mr. Gibson and the prince upstairs.

At the top of the stairs was a long hallway with several doors. There was also another stairway up to a third floor. They went down the hallway to a room on the end. Mr. Gibson took a deep breath and then opened the door. He entered the room, followed by Prince Kung and Inspector Gong. The prince's guard waited outside the room.

The scene was shocking. The woman, quite young, was lying on the floor in a pool of her own blood with an arrow sticking out of her chest. Her eyes were wide and her mouth open in a silent scream. Inspector Gong shook his head. He couldn't believe no one had bothered to close her eyes.

The girl was lying in front of a large window, but the window was shut and covered with a gauze curtain. The arrow had shattered the window, ripped through the curtain, and penetrated the girl nearly in the heart. It had been an incredible shot.

Inspector Gong pulled back the curtain a bit and looked outside. Across the street were the houses he had noted earlier. There were two houses, close together, where the killer could have stood. He had most likely been on the third floor or the roof of whichever house he used. He would need to speak to whoever owned those houses as well. Perhaps they housed the killer or would know who might have access to their house.

Prince Gong and Mr. Gibson were talking, but Mr. Gibson was becoming increasingly agitated. The inspector knew it was only a matter of time before they were kicked out. Even though Mr. Gibson most likely had frequent inter-actions with Chinese, he probably rarely had to answer to one.

The inspector kneeled down on his haunches to get a

better look at the body. The arrow was beautifully made. It was ornately carved and painted with gold and green. The fletching was made of bright green mallard feathers. It had to be possible to find out where such a unique arrow came from. To use such a specific weapon had to be a message. He needed to get a better look at it, perhaps the arrowhead held further clues...

"Out!" Mr. Gibson finally yelled. Another word that Inspector Gong easily understood.

The prince tried to placate him, but he was beyond placating now. If he dared to give orders to a prince, he obviously was past all sense of caring. The inspector, the prince, and the prince's men all traipsed downstairs and out the front door. They headed back to the main gate.

"What did you learn?" the prince asked through clenched teeth.

"Not enough," Inspector Gong replied. "We need to get the body to Dr. Xue, I need to examine the arrow, and I need to interview everyone in the house and hopefully the neighbors."

The prince scoffed. "None of which is likely to happen. These foreigners, they won't help us, even if it is in their best interest."

"What do you mean?" the inspector asked.

"They believe this should be handled internally since it happened in the legation. The Chinese want it handled by us, since a Chinese girl was the victim. It will go badly no matter what we do. If she was killed by a foreigner, we can't prosecute them. They would be prosecuted by the courts of their own country, which means they won't be prosecuted at all. If she was killed by a Chinese person, the people will think the killer was framed to protect the foreigners. Either way, this could get ugly. Tensions are high, and something like this could be like pouring oil on the flame and start an all-out war with the foreigners or rebel against the empress for not protecting the people against the 'White Devils'."

"We lose either way," Inspector Gong replied.

"Yes, but if we at least find out who did it," the prince said, "it could give me leverage. I could use it against the foreigners, to weaken their influence or to earn us some benefits. I could calm the fears of the populace, at least protect the empress and buy us some time."

"What are your orders, Your Highness?" the inspector asked.

"Find the killer," he said.

The inspector sighed. "In a walled city where I don't speak the language?" he asked, only half-joking.

"Well, you do know one person who speaks English, aside from me," the prince said.

"Who is that?"

"Lady Li."

Inspector Gong felt his breath hitch in his throat. Lady Li. She had helped him solve a case a couple of months previously. Her sister-in-law had been murdered in the Inner Court, the court of the ladies, in the Forbidden City. As a man, he could not be permitted into the Inner Court. However, Lady Li agreed to help him and went in his stead.

They had solved the crime and also discovered a passion for one another, spending one incredible night together in her quarters in the Forbidden City. But he had not seen her since her sister-in-law was formally laid to rest after they solved the crime. He wanted to see her, and had fought the urge to call on her many times, but nothing could ever come of it. She was Manchu; he was Han. Legally, they could not marry. Plus, she was a widow, and society dictated she remain as such for the rest of her life in reverence to her husband, even though she was only in her twenties. There were other considerations as well, but they all added up to the same thing—Lady Li was a woman he should stay away from, for both their sakes.

"Are you suggesting I ask Lady Li for her help?" Inspector Gong finally asked. "Again?"

"You worked well together last time," the prince said, without a hint of irony. The prince knew that Inspector Gong and Lady Li spent the night together, and he knew that they could not have a future together. So why was he so quick to encourage Inspector Gong to call on her?

"Is there something else going on here?" the inspector asked.

The prince shook his head. "It was only a suggestion. I suppose I could find another translator for you..."

"I didn't say you needed to do that," the inspector interrupted.

Prince Kung smiled. "I just think she can help you in more ways than as just a translator."

"What do you mean?" the inspector asked.

"Just call on her," the prince said. "You won't be disappointed."

2

*L*ady Li turned the letter over in her hands. At least this time Inspector Gong had the good sense to let her know he was coming, unlike the first time he came to her home. After her sister-in-law, Suyi, had been murdered in the Forbidden City, he practically barged into her home and demanded that she submit herself to the empress as a lady-in-waiting and help him find her killer.

Well, he had not been as brutish as that, but nearly so. And they did find the killer, though it was of little comfort. At least she had been able to bury Suyi with all the proper burial rites so she would not become a hungry ghost.

The last time she saw Inspector Gong was at Suyi's funeral. But things had been left so...unsettled between them. That had been weeks ago, and neither of them had found the courage or the means to bridge the gap that separated them.

At least Lady Li had her two daughters, her companion Concubine Swan, who had been her late husband's concubine, her mother-in-law Popo, and a household to run. But she was not supposed to know the comfort, or even the friendship, of a man again. If she was even seen in the company of a man, her reputation could be ruined. As a woman who could never remarry, her reputation might be of little importance, but she had her daughters to think about. Even though they were girls, since there were no male heirs, Lady Li's money and estates—which was all her husband's property when she married but was given to her upon his death—would be left to her daughters as dowries. That, along with their impressive pedigree, would make them two of the most eligible Manchu ladies in the empire as soon as they were of age in only a few years. It was not uncommon for elite Manchu girls to be married as young as thirteen years old. Lady Li's eldest daughter was the right age, the right pedigree, and had the right astrological numbers to be considered as a royal consort—perhaps even as the next empress. But should Lady Li ruin herself, she would also ruin any chances of her daughters making strong marriage ties.

Lady Li sighed. Of course she wanted to see Inspector Gong again. She had already given herself to him while she was undercover in the Forbidden City. But it could never happen again. Nothing could ever happen between them. She could not take a lover and risk her good name, and she could not remarry. Even if she cared nothing for her reputation, he was Han, and marriage between the Manchu and Han were forbidden.

She was reading the note again for the third time when she heard the front gate open. She looked up and saw her eunuch, Eunuch Bai, hurriedly entering. As a lady, Lady Li could not casually venture outside her family compound, so Eunuch Bai was her eyes and ears on the outside.

"What is going on out there," she asked him.

"A riot, My Lady," he said as he handed several parcels to the maids.

"Whatever for?" she asked.

"A young lady was murdered in the Foreign Legation, the British Quarter," he said.

"Why are the people rioting over that?" she asked. "Sounds like a British problem."

"She was Chinese," he said. "Zhao Weilin was her name. A maid in the home of a very wealthy merchant."

"Oh dear," Lady Li said knowingly. She handed Eunuch Bai the letter from Inspector Gong. "Do you think the murder has anything to do with this?"

He took the letter and read it quickly, then again more slowly. He cocked an eyebrow at her. "I did hear that Prince Kung and Inspector Gong were at the legation this morning. The incident has the potential to light the kindling that is unrest in the city. No doubt the prince is trying to stop an explosion before one starts. But that doesn't explain why Inspector Gong would be coming to you."

Lady Li shrugged and took the note back. "I suppose we will find out soon enough."

Eunuch Bai raised both eyebrows, but said nothing.

Lady Li rolled her own eyes. "Speak plainly. Your silence is loud enough."

"There will be no stopping the neighborhood gossips from speculating about his visit. When he was investigating the death of Suyi he had reason to be here. But now? This can only lead to trouble."

"My dear friend, of course you are right. But what can I do?" Lady Li asked innocently, even though they both knew there was something decidedly not innocent bubbling between Lady Li and Inspector Gong.

Eunuch Bai had been Lady Li's attendant since she first

entered the Forbidden City as a lady-in-waiting for the empress when she was only fifteen years old. He had been there for her when the whole court had fled for their lives to Jehol when the foreign powers attacks the Dagu Fort and marched on the Forbidden City. He had accompanied her when she left court and married her husband. He had comforted her after his death. He had proven himself her trusted friend for over a decade. She worried that part of his loyalty was wrapped up in his own improper feelings for her, something akin to love. But she did not feel that way about him, and he had never given voice to his feelings, so perhaps she was wrong. Regardless, he was her faithful servant and she his loyal lady, and they had been through too much together for anything to come between them, even someone as questionable as Inspector Gong.

"You are dismissed," she said with a mock air of superiority. "I must get ready for my guest."

"My Lady," Eunuch Bai replied with a small bow.

Lady Li then went to her quarters where a maid helped her dress in a silk embroidered chaopao, high pot-bottom shoes, and arrange her hair in the batou style atop her head.

She was just putting a little color on her lips when Eunuch Bai announced that the inspector had arrived. She felt butterflies swarm in her stomach and willed them to calm down. She slowly walked down the hall toward the sitting room where he was waiting for her, not that she could walk any other way in such shoes.

When she entered the sitting room, Inspector Gong rose from his seat to greet her. He was just as handsome as she had remembered. Maybe a bit more so. He could not suppress his own smile at seeing her, which gave his eyes a playful glint. He was clean-shaven, and his head was shaved in the front and his hair plaited down the back in the Manchu style that was required of all Chinese men no matter their ethnicity. He looked well, less stressed than when she had seen him previously.

"Lady Li," he finally said with a bow.

She gave a small bend of her knees and incline of her head in acknowledgement and motioned for him to retake his seat. She then took a seat nearby, but the tea table was between them.

"I am pleased to see you," she said. "Your note was rather vague, but I have the feeling your reason for your call is less grave than when you came to see me before."

"Less personal, perhaps," he said. "But no less serious."

"Is it in relation to the murder in the British Quarter?" she asked as she poured them some tea.

"Word travels fast," he said.

"There were people marching toward the riot outside my gate. I heard them when Eunuch Bai returned from his errands."

Inspector Gong nodded. "The crowd grows bigger by the minute. The girl's parents are mourning outside the gate to the legation. It is stoking the people's anger."

"And what is your role in this?" she asked.

"Prince Kung has instructed me to find out who killed the girl before all hell breaks loose between the people and the foreigners."

"That cannot be an easy task," she said. "The foreigners have their own police force. They will want to handle this internally."

"Exactly," he said, sipping the tea. He wondered how she knew so much about the foreigners. "If anything, Prince Kung should be handling the investigation. He knows the foreigners and their ways. He speaks English. But he is busy trying to keep the upper level diplomats and nobles happy and calm. He is trying to hold back the dam between both sides as long as possible so I can solve the crime."

"Do you think you can?" she asked as she refilled his teacup.

"Do you doubt my abilities?" he asked with a playful smirk that made her hand tremble slightly. She quickly placed the teapot back on the tray

"You have proven yourself resourceful in the past," she said noncommittally.

"I have a few leads I can pursue," he said. "I need to interview the girl's parents. And the murder weapon was quite unique. I think it will be easy to track down. But I worry it will not be enough. I can't examine the body or interview the people she lived with and worked for. I can't access the house where the killer probably laid in wait. I am not optimistic. But we must come up with some answer, some explanation that will keep the people from trying to storm the legation..." He shook his head, obviously distraught.

After he was quiet for a moment, Lady Li asked, "Why are you here?"

"What do you mean?" he replied.

"It sounds like you have a large job ahead of you. Why are you here with me? Should you not be out...investigating?"

He nodded. "Indeed. Prince Kung suggested I speak with you, but I don't know, really. I...I suppose I just wanted someone to talk to. Someone to bounce ideas off of. You were so helpful last time." He looked into his cup with a sense of defeat on his face.

Lady Li felt a blush rise to her cheeks. This was why she was developing feelings for this man. He did not see her as just a woman he could take to his bed, but saw her as a friend, a college, a confidant. He saw her as an equal.

Her husband had been similar. He too knew she could be valuable to him. As a diplomat, he knew that women could be a source of information and he had planned to use her to gain information from the wives of other diplomats. But he died so early in their marriage, they did not have much opportunity to put their plan into practice.

"Did I ever tell you that I can speak English?" she asked him, in English.

"What?" he asked, sitting up to attention.

"I said that I can speak English," she said in Chinese, a mischievous smile on her lips.

He smirked. "The prince did mention that. How did you gain this skill?"

"I think you forget that my husband worked for Prince Kung, and my father was a diplomat under the prince's father, the Daoguang Emperor," she said.

"But why would you speak English just because your husband worked for the prince?"

"British and American men are very different from Chinese men. They are greatly influenced by their wives. They consult with them and allow their opinions to influence their thinking."

"You are joking," Inspector Gong said nearly chuckling.

Lady Li shook her head. "Not at all. Why do you think the British Legation is so large? Their wives won't let the men leave them behind. Can you imagine Chinese diplomats traveling with all their wives and children and pets and cases of clothes and tea sets and dressing tables to the other side of the world for a temporary appointment? It is ridiculous. But that is how they are. That is why the legations have shops and schools and post offices and so on for all those families."

"Have you been to the legation" he asked.

"Many times," she said. "My husband believed that by having a wife who could be friends with the foreigners' wives, I could help influence the women in China's favor, and the wives would influence their husbands. I could go to their tea parties and listen to their gossip and tell him what their husbands were telling them."

"Your husband was training you to be a spy? Some kind of...espionage agent. Get inside and manipulate the foreign women and report back to him?" He was fully laughing now.

"You laugh, but don't underestimate the control foreign women have over their husbands. Women in the West have a lot of say in how their households and even their country is run. Britain has a queen who rules in her own right, don't forget."

"That is true," he said, regaining his composure. "So are you friends with the diplomats' wives?"

"I don't know," she said. "I only visited them a few times. I was only married for four years, and I was pregnant or in confinement for two of them. While he might have been able to bend the rules enough that I would be allowed out of my home to visit the ladies for tea once in a while, he could not bend them enough to let me be seen outside while I was with child. That would have been too much. I also couldn't leave the house during my year of mourning. After so long, it seemed strange to reply to their invitations."

"Do they still message you?" he asked.

She nodded and crossed the room to a small table. She opened one of the drawers and pulled out a small stack of letters. "I don't receive invitations very often, but some of the women there seem to still remember me."

Inspector Gong looked at the letters. He couldn't read them, but he recognized some of the Roman letters. They were definitely in English. "Lady Li," he said, "I think it's time you accepted these invitations."

"And do what?" she asked.

"Find out what you can about the girl and her death. This has to be the talk of the town in there. Maybe you can interview the family she worked for. The neighbors even. If you could encourage them to let us investigate, even release the body to us, that could change the tide of the investigation."

"But...why would they listen to me?" she asked, incredulous. "Didn't they nearly throw Prince Kung out of the legation? A prince! *The* prince. The one man trusted by foreigners and Chinese alike. Why would they listen to me if not him?"

"As you said, the women are different," he said. "He didn't talk to the merchant's wife. And she was definitely hiding something."

Lady Li sighed and paced the room. She was exhilarated by the chance to help, but terrified as well. She had nearly been killed in the investigation in the Forbidden City. She only found out who the killer was by accident really. This sort of investigation would require so much more finesse. And not only to question those involved, but he wanted her to persuade the family to cooperate? She shook her head.

"I don't know," she said. "It...it is so much to ask. I wouldn't know what I was doing."

"I know I am asking a lot," he said. "But you speak English, can get into the legation, can speak with the women. That is more than I can do. Anything you find out will be more than we knew before. I have faith in you."

"Who is the family?" she asked. "Who did the girl work for?"

"A Mr. Gibson and his wife. They had the largest house on the street I think."

"Gibson?" Lady Li asked. She took the stack of letters from Inspector Gong and rifled through them. She found one in particular and held it up. "She just wrote to me two weeks ago."

"Are you going to reply?" Inspector Gong asked.

She hesitated for a moment, but then she nodded.

"I'll do it," she said.

3

_I_nspector Gong was glad to have the aid of Lady Li, but he did not know just how much help she could be. Would the foreigners even admit her into the legation now, with tension so high? If they did, why would they take her words into account? Would they tell her anything of use? Even though he had his doubts, at least they had a plan to try. But the inspector was not without his own work to do.

With half a dozen of his own men, the inspector returned to the main gate of the Foreign Legation. The crowd had grown considerably, yet no violence had broken out. While half of the crowd seemed ready to attack with only the slightest provocation, the rest of the people appeared to only be watching, waiting to see what would happen.

When the inspector arrived, he could feel the tension increase. The people watched him closely, wondering if he were there to support the crowd or disperse it? Would this be the match that ignited the tinder of war?

The inspector had ordered his men not to harm the

people or use excessive force. They were merely to act as a barricade between the people and Inspector Gong. But the vast crowd didn't know that. Hopefully the mere presence of the guards would keep the people from escalating the situation.

The people parted ever so slightly, just enough for Inspector Gong and his men to shoulder their way through the crowd and make their way to the dead girl's parents, who were still publicly mourning their daughter.

Inspector Gong had to speak loudly for his voice to carry over the noise. "Zhao Laoye. Zhao Fuwen," he said. "I am Inspector Gong. I have been ordered by Prince Kung to investigate your daughter's death."

"Murder!" the girl's father yelled. "She didn't just die! She was murdered!"

The crowd growled their agreement.

"I don't disagree," Inspector Gong said. "But to find the killer, calmer heads must prevail. Will you speak with me?"

"What good will it do?" the old man asked. "There will be no justice for her. You can't arrest a White Devil for killing a Chinese girl, can you?"

Again the crowd erupted with jeers. One of the inspector's men stepped forward, as if he was going to punch the old man for his insolence. It was as though every person present held their breath to see what would happen. But Inspector Gong placed his hand on the man's shoulder and pulled him back. He then turned back to the old man.

"Come talk to me, uncle," he said, which was a polite way to refer to an older fellow even if he wasn't a relation. "Help me find out what happened to your precious daughter."

At this, the girl's mother nodded to her husband and

stood. She swayed a bit on her tiny bound feet, but quickly found her balance.

"There is an inn nearby we can talk at," Inspector Gong explained. "Let me buy you some food. You must be starving."

"Nothing fills an empty stomach like grief," the father said, but he headed toward the inn anyway, followed by his wife.

Inspector Gong nodded to his men. Two of them were to escort him and the elderly couple to the inn while the others worked to disperse the crowd. Without the mourning parents there as a rallying cry, he hoped the rest of the people would lose interest and head home.

The inn was sort of like a tavern, with rooms to rent, alcohol to drink, and food to eat. There were also people gambling and women soliciting their services. In one corner, two men were playing the pipa and the erhu for tips. Inspector Gong ordered a round of fried noodles for himself and the dead girl's parents and a pot of tea.

"So, where are you from?" the inspector asked as they waited for their food.

"Right here in Peking," the father said.

"Really?" the inspector asked, dubiously. Few people were actually "from" Peking.

"Well," the old man hedged. "My family was from Kwangsi Province. But during the Taiping Rebellion, we fled. You know it?"

Inspector Gong nodded. "I do. I was in the Hunan Army at the time. Kwangsi is beautiful."

"The Yao, the Taiping, Jintian, the war with the foreigners. Over and over again, our lands were ransacked and our sons killed. We couldn't stay. We came here for a better life. A peaceful life."

The food arrived. While Inspector Gong dug in, he noticed that the couple only picked at their food and sipped their tea.

"I am sorry for the loss of your daughter," he said. "Was she your only child?"

"Yes," the old man said quickly. "No other. Only one. We were depending on her to care for us in our graying years."

"How do you make a living here in the city?" Inspector Gong asked. Farming supported the people in the countryside, but in the city, one needed a trade to survive.

"I am a woodcarver," the father said with some pride. "I make the small, decorative panels many people use around their doorways. My wife, she makes lotus shoes."

Inspector Gong nodded. He didn't notice the girl having bound feet, but he hadn't had much time to examine her. "Did your daughter have bound feet?" he asked.

The old man shook his head. "We wanted to, of course. It is very proper. We wanted her to marry well. But when we first came to the city, the missionaries, they helped us. They helped us feed our...our daughter while we established ourselves. They taught her English. They would not allow us to bind her feet if we wanted her to go to their school."

Inspector Gong noticed that the father had stuttered a bit while telling his story, as if he was carefully choosing his words. He would only do that if he was trying to hide something, but he didn't want to pressure him now. He would try to find out more later.

"Tell me more about her," Inspector Gong said. "You said the missionaries taught her English."

"She was a very bright girl," the father said. "She could read and write English very well. And she could write Chinese. Had she been a boy, she could have been a scholar."

"Such a waste," Inspector Gong said as he refilled their teacups.

"Indeed," the father said as he nodded. "But she eventually got a job as a maid in that merchant's house. Not many Chinese girls can get such a good placement, or so we were told."

"Was it a good placement?" Inspector Gong asked.

"We thought so," the father said. "Until she was killed."

The mother coughed, chocking a bit on her tea, and gasped loudly. She had not said anything during their meal, but that was not uncommon. Most women would not have a conversation with a man who was not a member of her family. It was normal to let her husband speak on her behalf. But now, she began to cry and held a cloth to her eyes. She was not wailing for show now, but from real grief.

"They...they will not even give us her body," she stuttered through her tears. "Who is taking care of her? Who will wash her and brush her hair?"

The old man put his arms around his wife and looked at the inspector. "Can you help us?" he asked. "I know we will never get justice for our daughter, but will we at least be able to help her spirit rest?"

"I will do my best," the inspector said. "I have someone going to speak with the family she worked for. We will try to get the body released and find out what happened."

"Did you see our daughter? Do you have an idea of what happened?" the father asked.

Inspector Gong shook his head. Of course, he had seen the girl and knew how she died, but he didn't want to tell the father too much right now. Anything the father heard could influence his perception about what had happened to the girl. And he needed her parents to be as honest as possible, though he already had the feeling they were keeping things from him. Not that such a response was unusual. Most people had a few things about their lives they didn't want to become common knowledge. The trick was finding out if those secrets played a part in the death of the girl.

"Tell me more about your daughter. Did she have any enemies? Did she have a lover?"

The father shook his head. "No, nothing like that. She was a good girl."

Inspector Gong noticed that the mother was worrying her lower lip. "Zhao Fuwen?" he asked. "Is there something about your daughter I should know?"

She slowly nodded her head. "There...there is a boy. But they are in love. He also works in the legation. He is a...I don't know what they call it. Not a common coolie. He has to wear a suit and serve the family."

"You mean like a butler, or a footman?" the inspector asked.

"Something like that," she said.

"Why didn't you tell me this?" the father asked. "Was she whoring? Is that how she brought in extra money?"

"No!" the mother said adamantly, or as adamantly as she could in her low, humble voice she was used to using around her husband. "She was a good girl. But they were young and didn't want to leave their jobs. She didn't want you to worry because he lived in the legation too. She thought that if you knew, you would make her quit work. Make her come home so you could watch her."

"Well that would have been better than her ending up dead, yes?" the father yelled.

The mother's tears began to fall again at her husband's sharp tongue. Inspector Gong would usually stay out of a domestic squabble, but he still needed more information.

Though people did tend to be more honest when they were emotional.

"The boy," Inspector Gong interrupted. "What is his name? Where can I find him?"

"His name is Wang Bolin," the mother said, reducing her sobs to a sniffle. "I don't know where he lives, but I know he works very close to her. They would see each other often. I don't know his family."

The inspector wondered if he lived across the street from the girl. In one of the houses where the killer could have had a clear shot of the room where she died.

"I should be able to find him," the inspector said. "Were they quarreling, do you know? Would the boy have any reason to be upset with your daughter?"

The mother shook her head. "I don't think so," she said. "They loved each other, and they wanted to marry, but they both agreed to wait. He would have no reason to be angry with her."

"What about her employers?" he asked. "Mr. and Mrs. Gibson. Were they good employers? Did they treat her well?"

"As far as we know," the father said with a frown. "They always paid her on time and there were few language problems since she spoke English. She would often translate for the other servants as well, so she was well liked by her fellow workers."

"You mentioned she was bringing home extra money," the inspector said. "Where do you think that was coming from?"

The father hesitated. "Well, she said it was a bonus for her good work. Or because she made money writing letters for the other Chinese in the legation. Many can't even read or write Chinese you know. So if someone wanted to write to their parents or their husband or wife in the countryside or another city, she would do it for them and they would give her a few coins."

"But...?" Inspector Gong encouraged.

"But..." the father slowly said. "Now that you ask, I wonder if there was something we didn't know. I mean, someone killed her. There must have been more going on, yes?"

"I would have to agree with that," Inspector Gong said. "Of course, the killing may have been an accident. Or maybe she wasn't the intended target. Her death might not have had anything to do with her at all."

The father scoffed. "But you don't think that is the case, do you?"

Inspector Gong couldn't hide a small smile. The father was clever. While it was a bit endearing, it could also mean he was hiding more than Inspector Gong thought. He might have to look deeper at this innocent-seeming old timer.

"I...think I need to examine all possible scenarios," he said. "I will do my best to find out what happened to your daughter. I cannot promise you more than that."

"We cannot hope for much more," the father said. "When it comes to the Foreign Devils, there is no justice. They can come into our country, set up camp in our capital, burn our palaces. And what do we do? Give them more land! More treaties! Let them sell more drugs to our people!"

He was referring to the second war with the British over opium about eight years before. The imperial family had to flee the Forbidden City after the foreign powers attacked the Dagu Fort. After the war, several treaties were imposed upon China as punishment, which included fines, the loss of land, the right to import opium, and the creation of the legation inside Peking itself, in the shadow of the Forbidden City. The legation was considered foreign soil, and its occupants were treated as if they were living in their home country and were not subject to China's rules, laws, or customs. This created much friction between the foreigners and locals, who thought the foreigners were given special protection and privileges that were denied the local Chinese. Many Chinese resented that the foreigners were treated almost as royalty, instead of interlopers.

"I understand your frustration, your anger," Inspector Gong said. "First you were routed out of your home in Kwangsi by rebels. And now, your own daughter killed by the foreigners. But you must give me time. If there are riots, or if the foreigners feel threatened in any way, they won't work with me. Won't let my informants inside their walls, their homes. Do not go back to the gate. When you leave here, go home. I will come to you as soon as I learn what happened to your daughter."

"So those bastards' comfort is more important than my suffering?" the father asked. "Now, I cannot even mourn my daughter because the foreigners might feel scared? They should feel scared! This is China!"

The inspector reached out and put his hand on the old man's shoulder to calm him down.

"Just give me time," he said gently. "That's all I ask. Let me find your daughter's killer. Then we can decide what to do."

The man glared at the inspector, but once again, his wife demonstrated that she held more power over him than he would like to admit. She silently placed her hand on his knee and nodded. He calmed down considerably.

"Find out who killed our daughter, Inspector," he said.

Inspector Gong nodded. He stood to leave and paid the

innkeeper for the food and tea. He walked outside and his men followed him. He looked at the gate of the legation and noticed that the crowd had indeed dispersed, for now anyway. There were still more people hanging around than normal, and the gate was closed, the foreign guards tense.

The rest of his men came over to his side. They seemed a bit out of place now that the street was relatively quiet, so he let them attend to other duties.

He hoped that the dead girl's parents would return home like they promised and not rouse the crowd again. Lady Li had said that it was already too late in the day to call on Mrs. Gibson. She would have to wait until tomorrow.

He hoped the calm would hold that long.

4

*B*y the time Inspector Gong had left for the day, it was already much too late for a social call, according to British etiquette, so Lady Li would not be able to call on Mrs. Gibson until the next day.

She tried to recall what she knew about the woman, and, sadly, it wasn't much. Lady Li had only been to visit with the legation ladies a few times and was always surprised when she still received notes from them. She wondered if the ladies even realized she was receiving invitations or if their maids were just sending the notes to everyone in their address book.

No, that was a poor attitude to have. She needed to think that Mrs. Gibson actually wanted her to visit. She had to pretend they had been friends. If she went there with a defeatist attitude, she would be dismissed immediately. She had to affect an air of confidence, of familiarity.

She knew that Mrs. Gibson was married to a British general turned merchant. He had been to China several times when he was in the military and knew it was an excellent source of business. When he retired from the military, he was still young enough to embark on a new career and had decided to make China his permanent home, more or less, and had moved his family to the legation.

The Gibsons were one of the wealthiest families in the legation, and Mrs. Gibson was someone the other ladies tended to see as their leader, their rock, the sun around which their social lives circled. She knew everyone and everything that was going on, both in the legation and out of it. She was so knowledgeable about the news and gossip of London you would think she still lived there even though she only visited every couple of years. She also had a surprising grasp on the news and politics of wider Peking. She had a son who was currently in the military and serving in India and a daughter in her late teens who still resided with them.

Lady Li had no idea how Mrs. Gibson would feel about the girl being murdered in her home. Would she be scared? Annoyed? Sad? She also didn't know how she would be received when calling at such a time. She needed something to catch Mrs. Gibson's attention. Something that would make her invite Lady Li into her home and visit with her, even if she was not in the mood for social calls. She decided to ask her Eunuch Bai for help.

"Yes, My Lady?" he asked with a slight bow of his head.

"You know far more than I do about what is going on around the city," Lady Li said. "Is there anything going on in the legation, besides the murder of the girl?"

Eunuch Bai hemmed and hawed for a moment as he considered this. Eunuchs always traded in information. It was one of the main reason they were so valuable, and why many people did not trust them. They made up their own subset of society, and the secrets within it were not well known to most people on the outside, but one could usually tap into it, for the right price. Lady Li paid Eunuch Bai enough already that she did not need to bribe him for information, but there were still things he would rather keep close to his chest than share.

"Anything specific?" he asked.

"Something I can share with Mrs. Gibson that would help me gain her trust," Lady Li said. "A bit of tit for tat, if you will."

"You know there are no eunuch servants in the legation," he said. "The foreigners wouldn't be able to stand it."

"I am aware," she said with a nod. Foreigners would never hire cut men or bound foot girls. Though she had heard that eunuchs were not only found in China but some places in the west as well.

"So there is little I can tell you specifically about the goings on in the legation," he continued. "But you know that tension with the foreigners is high, especially with regards to the trade ports."

"Always," Lady Li said.

"According to my sources at the foreign ministry, customs is going to completely shut down the foreign ports in three days' time," he said. "They are going to call it a 'surprise inspection.' They are planning on shutting down the port for at least a week, maybe longer, depending on how things play out over the girl's death."

"That's impossible," Lady Li said. "China doesn't have the authority to close the foreign ports."

"This isn't coming from China," he explained. "Not directly anyway. The British customs official, Commander Hart, is going to issue the order himself."

"Why?" Lady Li asked, aghast. "That will hurt the British as much as the Chinese, if not more so, if they can't get their goods out."

"But it will please the Chinese, could calm tensions, at least for a little while. I heard Prince Kung asked it as a personal favor, both to please the empress and to keep any possible killer from escaping on any of the ships. You know Commander Hart is very careful when it comes to keeping the Chinese officials happy."

"So I've heard," she said with a grimace. Commander Hart was a bit of a controversial figure in the city. Too British for the Chinese; too Chinese for the British. He walked a thin line and never really earned the full trust of either country, but just enough that he was preferable to anyone else. "But what does this have to do with Mrs. Gibson?"

"Her husband has a ship scheduled to sail in four days' time," he said with a knowing raise of his eyebrow.

"So they aren't planning on telling the ship owners beforehand?" Lady Li asked.

"If they did, the shippers would all sail early and there would be no one to inspect, no ships to detain."

"But if Mr. Gibson was to just happen to sail early..." she said.

"Nothing suspicious about that," Eunuch Bai replied.

"Thank you so much, Eunuch Bai," Lady Li said. She started to turn away, but then she heard him clear his throat. "Yes?"

"I would not want you think that just because I am helping you that I approve of Inspector Gong," he said plainly. "He shouldn't be coming here. And he certainly should not be getting you involved in such a sordid affair."

"He helped solve Suyi's murder," she said. "I can't just turn him away when he calls. And he didn't ask for my help, I offered."

"All the worse," he said. "That man is a bad and dangerous influence."

"I think I am quite capable of making my own decisions," Lady Li said, crossing her arms.

"Indeed you are," Eunuch Bai said, a little more softly. "Which is why he is so dangerous. He...inspires you. Gives you courage."

"And that is a bad thing?" she asked, nearing laughter.

"In a world where one wrong move could ruin your reputation, and that of the entire family?" he asked. "Yes, it is."

She understood his meaning. Without Inspector Gong's encouragement, she wouldn't be so eager to go running off toward the scene of a murder, or allow an unmarried man to call on her so casually. It was dangerous. She had her daughters to think about. One wrong move and her daughters could end up completely unmarriageable, at least to someone of their class.

"I know you speak from the heart, Eunuch Bai," she said. "That you are only looking out for my welfare, and that of my daughters. I appreciate having someone in my life who worries about me so."

"But...?" Eunuch Bai asked, knowing that something more was coming.

"But," she continued, "I want to do this. I need to do this. I need to feel useful. I have to do something more to fill my days than sew clothes and order vegetables."

"You do have more," he said. "You have two wonderful daughters to raise."

"For how much longer?" she asked. "First Daughter is six years old. I went to the Forbidden City when I was fifteen. I have less than..." She stopped for a moment as she felt tears welling is up. "I have less than a decade left to spend with her. And Second Daughter is only two years younger. Women as young as thirteen have been called to serve at the palace. You know this.

"What am I to do when they are gone? What will fill my days? What will I have to look back on?"

"You think you will still be solving crimes ten years from now?" Eunuch Bai asked.

"I don't know," she said. "I certainly didn't think I'd be a widow at twenty-two. I didn't think my life would...I didn't think it would be like this."

"Like what?" Eunuch Bai asked.

Lady Li shook her head and walked to the latticed window of her room that looked out into the courtyard. She saw her mother-in-law, Popo, sitting in the sun watching the little girls play near the koi pond. She was laughing as they tried to catch the tiny frogs that were jumping along the edge of the pond. Popo had also been widowed young. Her only son had been Lady Li's husband, who had died only four years previously, and her only daughter had been Suyi, who had been murdered in the Forbidden City only a couple of months ago. Popo had spent most of her life alone and extremely ill. Lady Li had brought the old woman into her household so she could spend her final graying years with her granddaughters.

She also saw, sitting quietly to one side in the shade to protect her fair skin, Concubine Swan. Concubine Swan had belonged to Lady Li's husband and had no children of her own. She had been pregnant once, but when their husband, Lord Yun, died, she suffered a miscarriage. She had no other prospects. Lady Li knew that Concubine Swan often ate opium to help her cope with the long nights.

Her home, while full of people, was also full of sadness.

All the women in it were trapped and hopeless for the future.

Lady Li sighed and shook her head.

"Do not mistake my concern for lack of sympathy," Eunuch Bai said. "But since you have no father, husband, or elder brother to advise you, I feel it is my duty to be the word of reason."

"And do not think that because I ignore your advice that I do not appreciate it, Eunuch Bai," she said, turning back to him with a smile.

"As long as we are both clear," he said with a nod, and then left the room.

Lady Li shook her head and turned to her wardrobe. She so rarely left the house, she wasn't sure what she should wear. She dug in the very back of her closet and found something she hadn't worn in over four years—a British style walking dress. It was completely unlike a Chinese dress.

The only thing the two styles had in common was that they covered a woman from her chin to the floor and had long sleeves to her wrists. But while Chinese chaopaos and robes were straight without giving any hits about a woman's body and long bell sleeves, British gowns were extremely formfitting up top, as if to intentionally accentuate the bust, and a bustled skirt to accentuate the rear end. When Lady Li wore them, she felt simultaneously scandalized and confident. She was glad she would be riding in her sedan chair so not many people would be able to see her. Of course, styling her hair would be an issue as well. Her husband had talked about sending her maid to the legation to take a course in hair dressing to help her if she started regularly visiting the legation ladies, but after his death she thought it rather a waste. She might have to rethink that idea.

She called her maid to her room and together they pulled out her old corsets, crinolines, and walking boots. Some of the clothes needed a bit of repair work after sitting in boxes in the dark for so long. Some of the accent pieces were moth eaten, so the maid quickly repaired them with Chinese embroidered brocade. Of course, everything was horribly out of fashion, but there was no time to buy anything new. She would have to pay a visit to a French dressmaker while in the legation the next day.

The next morning, Lady Li's maid helped her dress. They decided to simply do her hair up in a bun and decorate it with several pins and clips. She would have to buy some hats at the shops as well. The boots were a trial as well. Lady Li couldn't bend over far enough to lace them up herself since the corset was so tight so the maid helped her with that but she was clumsy at tying them. She then had to practice walking around since the heel was more narrow than she was used to. She took a long look in a full-length mirror in her room and hardly recognized herself.

Lady Li finally took a deep breath, ready to head to the legation. Her maid accompanied her, since a lady, British or Chinese, would never venture out alone. Lady Li climbed into the sedan chair, which was carried by two chair bearers, and the maid trotted along beside her.

When she arrived at the legation, there was no crowd of protesters, thank goodness, but the area was quite busy. People were simply watching, waiting to see if something happened. The gates were still closed and there were several guards posted out front. As the bearers approached, a guard held up his arm to stop them.

"No Chinese allowed," he said.

Lady Li opened one of the flaps just a bit and handed him her invitation from Mrs. Gibson. "I'm a guest of Mrs. Gibson," she said firmly. "Open this gate at once."

"I see, ma'am," he said. "I can let you in, and your maid, but not the chair or the men."

Lady Li wasn't sure of the reasoning behind this, or if it were even true, but she decided not to make a fuss since they were at least allowing her inside. She opened the flap completely and her maid helped her out. She heard several gasps from people who were watching. She didn't think they knew who she was, but they would find out soon enough. She was certain that as soon as she was out of sight her chair bearers would be surrounded by curious onlookers.

She couldn't help but glance around herself to see if there was anyone she knew. Off to one side, near an inn, she saw Inspector Gong. He must have been watching the legation, looking for clues or suspicious people. He was not even trying to hide the fact that he was staring, with his wide eyes and his mouth agape. She felt her cheeks go hot as she remembered how shapely the western clothes made her look, but then she remembered that he had already seen her naked, so she was glad he still found her attractive when she was fully clothed.

She smirked, tossed her head, and entered the legation as if she belonged there.

5

*I*t had been years since Lady Li had stepped foot in the legation, but not much had changed. It was still a world apart, as if someone had simply picked up a neighborhood in Russia, America, or even Holland and had dropped it right in the heart of Peking, only a stone's throw away from the Forbidden City.

She noticed that many people were staring at her as she walked through the legation. She doubted many Chinese ladies visited here, and now with the legation on high alert, they probably didn't have many Chinese within the walls at all. Indeed, as she looked around, she saw very few Chinese servants running around. Usually there would be dozens of Chinese men in women going about their business like in any other neighborhood in Peking. Buying food, ordering clothes, hauling firewood. But now, she only saw a few Chinese and foreign servants rushing about, not nearly enough to be meeting all the needs of the foreign home-owners. She wondered if the servants had been banned from the legation or if they were being kept indoors. Certainly the ladies and gentlemen of the legation would not be able to survive if their servants had been banned from the legation. Who would help them dress and serve them tea? Lady Li smiled to herself at how hypocritical of her it was to criticize the foreigners for having servants. Was she not now followed by a maid? Was she not carried here by two men? Still, at least her servants were fellow Manchu. She didn't hire people of another race to serve her as if the color of her skin naturally made her superior. She didn't even have any Han servants.

She shook her head to rid herself of such complicated thoughts as she approached the large house. She needed to focus on how she was going to approach Mrs. Gibson.

There were several uniformed police officers milling about outside the house, as well as several important-looking men in suits, possibly diplomats and policemen of some sort.

As she approached, one of the uniformed officers raised his hand. "Whoa there, miss. Where do you think you are going?" he asked her in English. Some of the other men scoffed, as if they thought she wouldn't be able to reply.

"That is *lady* to you," she replied, trying to sound stern but was immediately surprised by how accented her English was. She nearly put her hand to her mouth in shock. While she remembered how to speak English properly in her mind, she had not practiced her spoken English in years, and it showed. Thankfully, the men seemed surprised enough that she spoke English at all, so they didn't focus on her accent.

"I'm calling on Mrs. Gibson," she said, speaking slowly and clearly, and handed the guard her invitation letter from Mrs. Gibson. The letter was some months old, but it had invited her to call any time. Lady Li had decided that any time was now.

The officer looked over the letter and then handed it to one of the suited men.

"Lady Li," he said with a smile. "I'm afraid this is not a good time. The Gibson family is undergoing a very difficult time..."

"I know," she said, cutting him off. "That is why I am here. Mrs. Gibson is my dear friend, and she needs comforting in this trying time."

Of course, it was very possible that Mrs. Gibson had given the police orders to not admit anyone. In that case, invitation letter or not Lady Li would not be admitted. But after a moment, the officer motioned for her to follow him.

"Please, follow me," he said with a wan smile. "We will see if she is accepting callers."

Lady Li nodded. She looked up at the house while they proceeded up the front walkway. She noticed that a window above the door was boarded up. She looked at the houses across the street. They were all of a similar height. The killer must have been in one of those houses, or on one of the roofs. She wondered how one would gain access to the roof of a house. Would it be very easy to climb?

The officer knocked on the door and a white maid answered. He gave the maid the invitation letter and she disappeared inside for a moment. She quickly returned and opened the door wide.

"Please come in," she said. "The mistress will see you, Lady Li."

Lady Li held her head high and entered without a glance at the officer. Her own maid followed her in and shut the door behind her.

Once they were inside. Lady Li ordered her maid to wait in the hallway. The Gibsons' maid led Lady Li to a parlor on the left. Lady Li took a deep breath to steel herself before entering.

Mrs. Gibson stood and faced Lady Li as she entered, a look of surprise on her face. Mr. Gibson was also there, though he hardly looked friendly and only nodded when she entered.

"Lady Li," Mrs. Gibson said with open arms, her mouth slightly agape. "I can hardly believe you are here."

Lady Li went to her and the two gave a friendly, if slightly awkward, hug. "I do hope you can forgive me for staying away so long," she said.

"It is nothing," Mrs. Gibson said, waving a maid over to serve them tea, British style. She sat on the large plush sofa, pulling Lady Li down with her. Mr. Gibson also sat rather stiffly in a large wingback chair to the side, but still said nothing. "But where have you been? It has been years," she asked.

"I have been at home, mostly," Lady Li said. "After the death of my husband, Chinese windows are required to go into a year of mourning. We are not allowed to do...well, anything really," she explained.

Mrs. Gibson nodded in understanding. "We have similar traditions. Though I doubt they are as strict as yours."

"Indeed," Lady Li agreed. "Well, after a year, I just thought I had been away so long, it felt awkward trying to reach out again, so I just didn't. I am so sorry. I hope you can forgive me."

"Of course, dear. Of course," Mrs. Gibson said and smiled as she poured some tea, sweetened it with sugar, and then cooled it with cream. She offered a cup to Lady Li.

Lady Li accepted the tea and did her best to stomach it, though she knew the milk would upset her stomach later.

"I am surprised you called now, after such a long absence," Mrs. Gibson hinted.

"But of course," Lady Li said. "I heard of your troubles with the maid. I had to come and see if you were all right. And if you needed any help. This cannot be an easy situation to balance with the Chinese authorities or the girl's parents. A clash of cultures, if you will."

"How...kind," Mrs. Gibson said as though unsure if Lady Li was there to be genuinely helpful or if she was just there wanting to stick her nose in where it wasn't wanted.

"And with the troubles at the port," Lady Li continued. "It must be a stressful time for your husband as well." She didn't make eye contact, but said this as though it was common knowledge.

"What troubles at the port?" Mr. Gibson asked, his first words since she arrived.

"Oh, that Commander Hart is planning to close the port in two days' time," she said. "There is going to be some sort of inspection and none of the ships will be allowed to leave for who knows how long."

"What the devil are you on about?" Mr. Gibson exclaimed, leaning forward.

"Henry!" his wife gasped. "Language."

"It's quite all right," Lady Li said. "I know it must be disconcerting. You have a ship leaving soon, yes?" she asked Mr. Gibson directly.

"I do," he said. "In just three days! It's nearly loaded already, tons of goods. Months of work. One of our biggest shipment of the year. If that shipment is delayed...Damn!" He stood and tossed his newspaper to the floor. "Damn that Hart!"

"Mr. Gibson," Lady Li said calmly. "Is it possible to leave a day early? Can your captain be ready?"

"I think so," he said. "It will take some work, and the men won't be happy, but it could be done. Will Hart let us leave? Will he suspect I know about the inspection?"

"From what I have heard he won't stop any of the ships from leaving early. He doesn't want anyone to know what will happen, and if he prevents ships from leaving, that would cause suspicion. I wouldn't tell anyone why you are leaving. If all the ships tried to leave at once, Hart might close the port at any time. But if you can convince your captain to leave early, that would be the best solution to this problem."

"How...how do you know this?" he asked.

"My husband was a diplomat," she said, straightening her back and holding her chin up. "I still have my friends on the inside. Hart seems to think a surprise inspection would calm the situation, at least for a time."

Mr. Gibson scoffed. "Yes, well, we will see about that." He started to rush off, but then seemed to recall his manners. "Thank you, Lady Li, for the information. You have no idea how useful it is."

Lady Li knew exactly how useful she was being, but she smiled and nodded innocently. "Certainly, Mr. Gibson."

He left, and Lady Li turned back to Mrs. Gibson.

"That was..." Mrs. Gibson paused. Lady Li feared for a moment that Mrs. Gibson had seen the move for the manipulation it was. "...so kind of you, Lady Li," she finally finished.

Lady Li sighed with relief and reached over and touched Mrs. Gibson's hand. "It is nothing after the kindness you have shown to me over the years," she said, and she meant it. Mrs. Gibson had been very friendly to her back in the day, inviting her to socialize with the other ladies of the legation as if she was one of them. Lady Li began to regret cutting herself off from the woman over the years. She had so few friends. Perhaps some female friends, even foreign ones, would help with the oppressive loneliness she felt.

Mrs. Gibson leaned back and seemed to relax a bit on the sofa. "You have no idea how terrible it has been," she said.

Lady Li nodded in sympathetic agreement. "I am sure."

"That girl..." She shook her head. Lady Li stayed quiet, a technique she had learned from Inspector Gong. Once a person was ready to talk, it was best not to interrupt them. "It was so shocking. Right here, in my own home. I still can't hardly believe it." She sipped at her tea as her mind wandered. Lady Li noticed her hand was shaking slightly.

"What happened?" Lady Li asked.

"She was shot through the chest, but with an arrow. Can you believe it? Upstairs in the guest bedroom. Crashed right through the upstairs window. One of the other maids found her."

"An arrow?" Lady Li repeated. "How strange."

"Isn't it? Must have been some sort of freak accident. A ricochet from somewhere."

Lady Li wasn't so sure. She didn't think an arrow had the power to ricochet and still have enough speed behind it to crash through a window and kill someone. A bullet, maybe. But an arrow? She thought someone must have been aiming for the girl, but why? And from where? She would have to see who lived across the street.

"Were you home when it happened?" Lady Li asked. "I'm so glad it wasn't you or your daughter who was struck instead."

"Thankfully, no. We were not," Mrs. Gibson said. "We were at a show. The whole family. The London Theater

Company was staging a production of *Hamlet* nearby. So none of us were home."

Lady Li nodded. So not only were they not home, they were all together in public. So most likely none of them killed the girl. But one of them could have ordered it done while they were out of the house.

"How long had she worked for you?" Lady Li asked, wanting to find out more about the girl.

"Oh, a couple of years I believe," Mrs. Gibson said. "She will be hard to replace. Usually the Chinese servants can't speak English, so they just do menial tasks. But she was quite useful. I just gave her a raise. I was hoping she would stay on."

"Were you worried she was going to leave?" Lady Li asked.

"Possibly," Mrs. Gibson said. "She had a beau. If she got married, her husband and their families wouldn't let her remain in service."

Lady Li nodded. "It is hard to be in service and have a family."

"Well, it would happen eventually," Mrs. Gibson said. "She was pretty and smart. Someone would certainly snatch her up. But she seemed very grateful for the raise. I had the feeling...I think she needed the money."

"What makes you say that?" Lady Li said.

"Well, she never said anything, but she was always willing to take on more work for a bit of extra cash. She would do intricate embroidery work in the evenings for other ladies in the neighborhood. But as an only child, I am sure her parents depended on her quite a bit."

Lady Li nodded as she considered this. If the girl had a boyfriend and their relationship was serious enough that they were thinking of getting married, would he have felt slighted that she chose the raise and the job over him? Would the family have felt insulted enough to have her killed? It was possible.

"Do you know the boy?" Lady Li asked. "The beau?"

Mrs. Gibson shook her head. "No. I know he works somewhere in the legation, but I don't know his name."

At this point, Lady Li couldn't think of anything else to ask, so she just made pleasant small talk. She asked about Mrs. Gibson's daughter and if they had plans to travel during the cooler fall months. She told Mrs. Gibson about her own daughters and the recent death of her sister-in-law, Suyi. Before she knew it, a couple of hours had passed and it was time for lunch.

"I am so sorry for taking up so much of your time," Lady Li said as she stood to leave.

"Not at all," Mrs. Gibson said. "I quite enjoyed the chat. I do hope you will come again. You are always welcome in the legation."

At that, Mr. Gibson came back, striding right into the parlor still wearing his hat. "Lady Li!" he said loudly, making Lady Li jump. He stepped up to her and took her hand in both of his, shaking it vigorously. "Thank you for the information. I was able to get everything arranged to set the ship to leave early. And good thing too. It would have been a terrible blow if we hadn't gotten the goods to market as promised. Thank you. I mean it."

"Oh, of course," Lady Li said, though she was a bit unsure of what to do with her hand stuck in his grip.

He raised her hand to his mouth and kissed it. She gasped and felt her face blush deeply.

"I mean it," he said. "If there is anything I can do."

"Well..." She paused. She did have a request, but she was worried about the good faith she had just garnered from them both. But she also thought it might be good to capitalize on his excitement in the moment. "The dead girl, the maid...I heard that her body had not been released to her parents. You know how important death rites are to us. When my own kin recently died, the police also kept her body for so long, we were worried we wouldn't be able to bury her before her soul became trapped on this side and she became a hungry ghost. I know this is police matter, but if there is anything you can do..."

The Gibsons stood silent for a minute, and then Mr. Gibson burst out laughing. "Hungry ghost!" he exclaimed. "Oh I forget what silly superstitions you people have." He continued laughing, and even Mrs. Gibson couldn't stifle her giggles completely.

Lady Li felt her anger rise up. Who were these people to laugh at her? Did they not also have superstitions? Did they not bury their dead facing east? Did they not cover mirrors? But she forced herself to be calm and even chuckle a little herself. She needed to remain in their good graces if she wanted anything from them.

"Yes," Lady Li finally said. "I know it sounds silly. But her parents are simple country people. So if you could..."

"Yes, yes," Mr. Gibson said, wiping tears from his eyes. "I'll see it done. Don't worry."

"Thank you so much," Lady Li said, trying not to grit her teeth. "It will mean so much to them."

Mr. Gibson nodded and finally let go of her hand. Mrs. Gibson led her back to the entryway, where Lady Li's maid was still waiting. Lady Li turned and gave Mrs. Gibson another hug before heading out.

"I mean it," Mrs. Gibson said. "Do come back."

As Mrs. Gibson's maid opened the door and they stepped out onto the porch, Lady Li motioned to the houses across the street. "Who lives over there?" Lady Li asked. "I seem to have forgotten."

"Oh, well you wouldn't know the family straight across," Mrs. Gibson said. "The Belvederes just moved in about a year ago. But next to them would be the Highcastles. You do remember Lady Highcastle, don't you? She answers directly to the queen. Can you believe it? Queen Victoria is quite interested in the goings on around here, and even though she has official reports by the generals and the diplomats, she apparently loves to hear about things from a woman's perspective from time to time. Can you believe such a thing?"

Lady Li could, actually. China was currently ruled by an empress, much the same as Great Britain was. She had served the empress as a lady-in-waiting for several years. She knew that even though the empress had countless official court ministers, her real advisers were often the ladies of the Inner Court.

But did that have anything to do with the death of a maid? Lady Li doubted it, but she would have to find some way to visit with Mrs. Belvedere and Lady Highcastle.

6

*A*s always, Lady Li looked stunning. But in that tight British style gown, Inspector Gong couldn't control his arousal. He was glad he was dressed in a loose Chinese-style robe and not the constricting trousers like a British man. Oh the things he wanted to do to that woman...

On one hand, he was surprised at how easily she gained access to the legation; but on the other, he was not surprised at all. She had proven herself quite resourceful it the past. It was one of the reasons he had turned to her now. That and he had been growing desperate for a reason to see her.

He couldn't get her off his mind. He had abandoned his regular trips to the flower houses after meeting her. It somehow felt wrong to return to prostitutes after the amazing night he had spent with Lady Li in the Forbidden City. He wasn't sure why. He knew he had feelings for her. Had things been different, he would probably try to court her. But he couldn't. Why should he deny himself the touch of any woman because he couldn't have the one he really wanted? It didn't make sense.

Yet he couldn't shake the fantasy of having her in his life. Of course, he also wanted her in his bed, but more than that he appreciated her company. For the first time in his life, he could imagine having a wife. Someone he could come home to, share his day with, and ask advice of.

But he couldn't think about that right now. Now, he needed to focus on this case. The prince was worried the people could revolt, attempt to storm the legation. Inspector Gong thought that was highly unlikely, but it was true that many people disliked the foreigners holding such a prominent place in Peking, both physically—right in the shadow of the Forbidden City—and socially. The foreigners, even if they left the legation and ventured into Peking proper, were given special treatment. They were not beholden to Chinese law. They were governed by the laws of their home country, no matter where in China they were or how severe the crime. It was not uncommon for foreigners to kill Chinese people and simply be returned to their homeland, more for their protection from the wrath of the locals than to actually see justice in their own courts. Though that usually happened in more rural places. Here in Peking, the foreigners might engage in unscrupulous business practices or beat their housemaids, but they didn't murder. The murder of a young lady was a crime against the dignity of the Chinese that could not be ignored.

He milled around outside the gate of the legation and waited for Lady Li to return. It was a grueling two hours. Finally, she emerged, followed by her maid. He quickly crossed the street toward her.

"Lady Li," he said with a bow.

"Inspector Gong," she replied, inclining her head.

"Would you care to join me at the inn nearby," he asked. "So we can have a chat."

"I certainly would mind," she replied. "I have some shopping I must see to before I return home. And I certainly could not be seen in a public house."

"Shopping?" he asked. "Shopping is more important than finding the girl's killer?"

"It is part of the investigation," she explained. "The foreigners have strict social rules, just as we do. I look a fright in this old, rotting frock. If I wish to call in the legation again, I must look the part."

He sighed but accepted that she had a point. He was asking her to go undercover. She had to blend in with the other ladies. Well, as much as a Chinese woman could anyway.

"Do I have permission to call on you at home, then?" he asked.

"Indeed," she said with a small smile. "Midafternoon."

*W*hen he was led to Lady Li's receiving room, he was disappointed to see she was once again dressed in her Chinese chaopao. He had hoped to have more glimpses of her in that tight western gown.

She stood to greet him. "Inspector Gong."

"Lady Li."

She waved Eunuch Bai away, leaving them alone in the

room, but he knew the eunuch was probably watching and listening from a spyhole nearby.

They sat in chairs on either side of a tea table.

"So, what did you learn?" he asked as she poured him a cup of tea.

"Probably nothing of use," she said humbly. "Except that the immediate family—Mr. and Mrs. Gibson and their daughter—were not home on the night of the murder. They were at the theater, so there are probably many people who can account for their whereabouts."

"So they have alibis then," he mused.

"They have what?" she asked.

"We call it an alibi, when someone says they were somewhere and another person can vouch for them," he explained.

"Oh, I see," she said. "Well, did you have reason to suspect them anyway?"

"Other than the fact that the girl was murdered in their home?" he asked. "No."

"I suppose that would make them the first suspects," she said. "But Mrs. Gibson said she was quite fond of the girl. She had recently given her a raise to convince her to stay on instead of getting married. She said that she was being courted by a young man who also worked in the legation."

"Did she know who he worked for?" he asked.

"No, I'm sorry," she said. "But it is possible she jilted him after Mrs. Gibson gave her the raise. She said that the girl always seemed in need of money. That she would take on extra embroidery work from the neighbors. Do you think she did it to support her parents? Are they unable to care for themselves?"

"Her parents still work," he said. "They seemed in fine health. They both have a trade. Her father is a woodcarver and her mother embroiders lotus slippers. They also get help from the missionaries. That is how the girl learned English, and why she didn't have bound feet."

"So if her parents weren't solely reliant on her to support them, why else would a young lady need money?" Lady Li wondered aloud. "She wasn't saving for a wedding since she chose the job over the boy. So what was it?"

"Could be any number of things," Inspector Gong said. "Could be nothing. Young women like to shop. Maybe she just wanted a new dress so she could look fashionable while she walked around the legation." He raised an eyebrow at her.

"Are you making fun of me?" she asked teasingly.

"I'm just imagining you in those fine new clothes," he said. Lady Li blushed. "Will I get another chance to see you in them?"

"Perhaps," she said. "I did enjoy my time with Mrs. Gibson today. I think I might visit her again."

Their eyes lingered on one another for a bit. It went unsaid that she was also enjoying her visit with Inspector Gong. He had the feeling that she had missed him as well.

He cleared his throat. "Or she could have been saving money for a more nefarious purpose. Perhaps she had a gambling problem or an opium addiction."

"How dreadful," Lady Li said turning back to her teacup. "Well, it was probably not opium. She wouldn't be able to work if her mind was in the clouds."

"You do have a point there," he said. "Maybe her parents know."

"If they do they probably won't tell you," she said. "They won't want to say anything that could show their daughter in a bad light."

"Well, that is true of almost everyone I interrogate," he said. "But I always get them to talk."

"Fortunately, I did get Mr. Gibson to agree to release the girl's body to them," she said.

"You did?" he asked, surprised. "How clever you are. How did you do it?"

"I cannot reveal all my womanly secrets to you," she said with a smirk. "But, stupid me, I did not ask where it was or how they would get it."

"Don't worry about that," he said. "Leave the gory details to me. Did you learn anything else of note? You were there an awfully long time."

"I don't think so," she said. "But I know one of the families who lives across the street from the Gibsons, in one of the houses where the killer could have been. I'll have to try to call on Lady Highcastle and see what I can find out."

"Good," he said. "But don't try to do too much too fast. You don't want to make yourself obvious."

"Well it didn't help that an investigator was waiting for me outside the legation," she said with a quirk of her eyebrow.

"Hmm, you are probably right about that," he said. "But I couldn't resist. I haven't seen you in so long." He paused. "I missed you," he finally dared to say softly.

The playful smile dropped from her face and she looked away. At first, he thought he had offended her. But then she stood and walked to the wall. Inspector Gong stood as well, expecting her to dismiss him. Instead, she moved a small table with a vase on it slightly to the left. She then walked over to Inspector Gong and put her arms around his neck.

"I missed you too," she said in nearly a whisper.

Inspector Gong pulled her to him and kissed her

passionately. He felt his desire rise and he ran his hands over her body.

"Oh, woman," he groaned. "I need you."

"And I you," she said softly. "But...we cannot. In the Forbidden City, I was free. But here, even now I am watched. I moved the vase so he cannot see us, but I am sure he is still listening."

"He is your servant," he said. "So what if he knows? Order him to turn the other way."

"It is not that simple," she said. "It is a lot to ask of him. And it would grant him immense power over me. I trust him, but who knows what the future will bring. Besides, other people saw you arrive, the neighbors. You should leave soon."

Inspector Gong turned away and rubbed his head in frustration. Then he turned back and gently touched her cheek. "We will find a way," he said. "We will find a way to be together."

"It is a lovely dream," she said. "But for now, you have a crime to solve."

$\mathcal{H}$e didn't know how she did it, but Inspector Gong was learning to not question Lady Li's ways. Somehow she had gotten the foreigners to release the girl's body. She didn't have the details of the exchange, but he was able to work things out easily enough. The foreigners weren't doing anything with the body anyway besides letting it decay in their custody.

He had Prince Kung send a message to the chief of the British police force in the legation instructing him to release the body to Inspector Gong. When Inspector Gong arrived at the legation the next day, they released the body to him with no problems. He was surprised the body was in nearly the same condition she had been in when he saw her. It didn't look like anyone had attempted an autopsy, which he thought was strange. The girl was murdered in the home of the wealthiest man in the legation. Did they not want to solve the crime? If not, why not?

He had the body sent to Dr. Xue, Inspector Gong's trusted friend and a doctor of Chinese medicine. He some-times examined bodies for Inspector Gong in the back room of his medicine shop. He gave the doctor a few hours to conduct his preliminary exam and called on him in the afternoon.

"The cause of death was an arrow to the chest," Dr. Xue proudly proclaimed when the inspector arrived.

"I know that," Inspector Gong said.

"Oh," the doctor said, disappointed. "I thought you had sent me an easy case."

"It probably is easy enough," Inspector Gong said. "I know the cause of death. The arrow was still sticking out of her when I first examined the crime scene. I was just hoping you'd be able to tell me if there was anything else about her I should know."

"Hmm," the doctor mumbled to himself as he pulled the sheet back, revealing the splayed open body of the girl. "Young, healthy. No poison this time," he said, referring to the case of Lady Li's murdered sister-in-law from a few months back.

"That's good," Inspector Gong replied. "But it doesn't really help us."

"Well, she was also with child," the doctor said. "About three months gone."

"Really?" the inspector asked, raising an eyebrow. "You are sure?"

"When you know what to look for, the signs are easy enough to spot."

"Would she have known?" Inspector Gong asked. He really knew very little about the particulars of childbearing.

"Probably," the doctor said. "It's possible she didn't know. Young women, they don't always know the ways of the world, but many women notice certain...changes after two or three months. She should have at least suspected something wasn't right."

"Lady Li talked to the woman's employer. She was a maid in the legation," the inspector explained. "She had just accepted a raise. The employer was under the impression she was going to keep working. But if she had known she was pregnant, she wouldn't be able to keep working."

"Maybe she had planned to get rid of it," the doctor said.

"Would she have been able to do that?" the inspector asked, once again showing his ignorance when it came to things women and children related.

"Of course," the doctor said. "Up to six months she could have taken care of it rather safely. After that, though, most doctors who take care of that kind of thing would probably advise her to give birth and then get rid of it."

"They would encourage murder?" Inspector Gong asked, raising an eyebrow.

"Nah," the doctor said with a wave of his hand. "Just abandon it somewhere. Leave it in Heaven's hands. Or she could have left it with the missionaries. They seem to specialize in taking in foundlings."

"She did have a connection with one of the missions," Inspector Gong mused. "She went to school at one. But would she have been able to hide a pregnancy, and a birth?"

"Some women can hide it," the doctor said. "Some women don't gain much weight when they are pregnant. And if their clothes are loose enough, sure. The birth itself, that could be much more difficult."

"Where are her clothes?" the inspector asked, looking around the room.

"Here," he said walking over to the simple wooden casket she had been delivered in. It looked as though she had only been wearing a simple green sleeping robe at the time and a few underclothes. It was late at night when she had been found. She must have been ready for bed.

He thought back to the room she had been found in. He had only had a few minutes examine the scene, and he spent most of it examining the girl, so he tried to remember what he saw of the room. The details were fuzzy, but he distinctly remembered seeing a bed, a large bed with heavy wooden posts. All of the furnishings in the room looked large and high quality. A room too fine for a servant. Why would she be walking around the house and in a bedroom that wasn't hers in her sleeping garments?

"Was the murder weapon included with her things?" he asked.

The doctor shook his head. "No, and no personal items. Just the body."

Inspector Gong let out a long exhale. No personal items. How cold were these British people? Surely they would know that her parents would want what few things she had. Wouldn't they want them if they had been in their shoes? Even if she only owned a few cheap garments, it was all they had left of her. Who knows what Lady Li had given them to get the body; would she have anything left to give to secure her personal belongings? How much were these people going to make her bow and scrape to get them?

To say nothing of finding the arrow. It was unique enough that Inspector Gong would remember it, but actually having the evidence in hand would be more useful to him.

"She had a boyfriend," the inspector said. "And he works in the legation too. If he was the father, why didn't she just marry him? Not like he was some penniless scrapper."

The doctor pursed his lips for a moment. "I can think of one reason why she wouldn't marry him."

Inspector Gong nodded knowingly. "If he wasn't the father."

The doctor nodded in agreement.

"But still, the boy probably wouldn't know he wasn't the father. Why not just claim he's the father, quit her job, and let him take care of her?" Inspector Gong asked.

"That's why you are the inspector, Inspector," the doctor said. "I don't pretend to understand people, especially women."

"Is married life no longer heavenly bliss?" the inspector joked. The doctor was an older man and only recently purchased a young wife for himself.

"You'll know, soon enough," the doctor said as he started to close the body of the dead girl back up.

"What do you mean?" Inspector Gong asked.

"I've heard that your mother has been making... inquiries," the doctor said slyly.

Inspector Gong groaned and rolled his eyes. "Nothing will come of it. She can ask around and pray at the temple all she wants, I won't agree to anything."

"Have you ever really defied your mother?" the doctor asked. "Really? Have you ever truly stood before her and told her you would not do as she asked?"

"No..." he slowly admitted. He and his mother had more of a silent agreement. As the youngest son, there had never been a real rush to get him married off. She had patiently allowed him free rein over his life. She let him join the army during the Taiping Rebellion. She then allowed him to work with Prince Kung, solving some of the most pressing cases around the city. She let him drink and whore and do whatever he wanted. His older brothers were already married with children of their own, so she had let him enjoy his bachelorhood for far too long. But even he couldn't defy his filial duty forever. Eventually he would have to marry and have children. It was the natural order of things and his number one duty as a son.

"Maybe she just thinks it is time," the doctor said. "I can't be the only one to have noticed a change in you lately."

"What do you mean?" Inspector Gong asked, playing dumb.

"Good thing you decided to be an inspector and not an actor," the doctor said as he started stitching up the girl. Inspector Gong couldn't help but wrinkle his nose as he watched the gruesome task. "You haven't been visiting the flower houses like before. And you've been drinking less. There's a...somberness about you," Doctor Xue explained.

"I've just...been busy," the inspector said. "I have a lot on my mind."

"A lot?" he asked. "Or just one thing? Or one person, I should say."

Inspector Gong stayed silent, neither confirming or denying the doctor's accusation.

"Is she someone your mother wouldn't approve of?" the doctor asked. "Is she a whore or from a poor family?"

"Not exactly," the inspector said. "But...we can't be together. Nothing can come of it."

"She's married?" the doctor asked.

Inspector Gong stayed silent. He let the doctor think he was right. It would be better than him figuring out the truth.

The doctor nodded. "Then maybe letting your mother make a match would be for the best. You've obviously changed your mind about staying a single man forever. You've at least been entertaining thoughts of marriage, yes? Well, how better to get over a woman you can't have than by taking a woman you can."

Inspector Gong sighed. The old doctor was probably

right. He needed to marry. And if he couldn't marry Lady Li, why not marry someone else? Maybe he could stop thinking about her so much if he had another woman waiting for him at home. His growing feelings for Lady Li were only going to lead to disaster. For one of them at least; possibly both of them.

"As always, you are full of wisdom, Doctor Xue," Inspector Gong said as he gave him the fist-in-palm salute. "And thank you for the information about the girl. Let me know if you discover anything else. I'll send her father to collect her."

Inspector Gong left a small pile of coins on the counter on his way out. He felt the need to call on Lady Li. He wanted to tell her about the girl being pregnant and ask her what she thought about it. Lady Li had two children. She might have some ideas about the girl's motives. But he walked slowly. He knew he shouldn't involve her further. He shouldn't keep seeing her. Dr. Xue was right, he should marry and leave Lady Li far behind him. Then why did he keep walking toward her home? Why did she draw him so?

He knew why. She was fascinating. No woman his mother found for him would ever be as interesting as Lady Li. Any woman his mother picked would just kneel and fawn. She would do embroidery work and have children. They wouldn't have anything in common and she wouldn't know anything about the wider world. He wouldn't be able to share his day with her, and she wouldn't be able to help him with his cases.

Any other woman in all of China would be a poor substitute for Lady Li.

8

*L*ady Li was anxious. She paced the floor of her sitting room, waiting for...something. She wasn't sure what. She hated being left in the dark. When she had helped Inspector Gong with a case previously, she was right in the thick of it. It had been her own family member who was the victim, and she was the one doing most of the investigating since Inspector Gong was barred from entering the Inner Court, the court of the ladies.

But now, she wasn't so intimately involved. She could only do as he asked and then give him the information, but there was little she felt she could do on her own. If she wanted to know anything else about the progress of the case, Inspector Gong had to be gracious enough to tell her, but she couldn't force him.

She hated giving him any power over her. She was above him socially, and as a widow, the head of her own household. Granted, in the great scheme of things, she was a rather insignificant person. But at least she didn't have to directly answer to any man. Any amount of power Inspector

Gong held over her felt as though she was losing the little bit of the autonomy she had.

But it was more than the case that had her frustrated. Inspector Gong had been out of her life for months. For both of their sakes, he should have simply stayed away. Yet here he was, back in her life. And she didn't want him to leave again. She wanted him to call on her, for any reason, related to the case or not. The one night they had spent together in the Forbidden City had reignited a passion in her she had almost forgotten had existed. She was now having trouble sleeping and was restless during the day. It killed to her to admit it, but she missed him. She wanted him. She wanted to find a way...

Eunuch Bai knocked on her door.

"Enter," she said.

"Inspector Gong," he announced.

Her breath hitched in her throat as he entered. He looked harried, rushed. His gaze was intense.

"Leave us," she somehow managed to say even though her throat was tight.

Eunuch Bai nodded and shut the door.

Inspector Gong stared at her, but he didn't speak. He didn't give her the required bow or state his intention. She also did not give him a curtsey or motion for him to take a seat. It was as if they were both frozen. Both wanting something they were unable to name.

Finally Inspector Gong walked over to the table with the vase and moved it in front of Eunuch Bai's peep hole. Then in only two quick strides, he was face to face with Lady Li. Still he did not speak.

Lady Li's breath quickened. Was this happening? "Wha...what are you..." she tried to ask, but the words died in her mouth. Inspector Gong took her face in his hands and kissed her. She closed her eyes and leaned into him. She opened her mouth and let him taste her.

He moved from her mouth to her neck and his hands roamed down her body. "I need you," he finally whispered.

She nodded, unable to reply. Her eyes darted around the room. It was small and only had some chairs for visiting and a desk where she did some paperwork and writing. There was no bed or couch or any other suitable large surface.

None of that seemed to matter to Inspector Gong. He pushed her against the wall and fumbled with his robe and pants as he unencumbered himself. He grabbed her hand and led her to his manhood. He was already fully excited, but he groaned at her touch.

He then began to pull up her chaopao and linked one of his arms under her knee, lifting her up to him. He had done this before. She was more used to the slow, sensual method of lovemaking, but she had to admit that the rough and urgent way he was taking her now was something she had fantasized about. Especially lately, since they could not be together and she had not come up with a plan to take him to her bed, she had imagined moments very similar to this, something quick, something passionate, something that didn't take long but would still meet their needs.

"Yes...yes..." she sighed as they joined together. She did her best to stay quiet, but she knew the walls were thin. There would be no way to keep what she was doing a secret from her servants, especially Eunuch Bai, but she could at least pretend she was being discreet.

Inspector Gong buried his face in her shoulder as he took her, doing his best to muffle his own groans of pleasure.

After only a moment, they had both reached the heights

of ecstasy, yet they continued to stand against the wall, breathing deeply, neither wanting the moment to end.

"Maybe...maybe now I will be able to focus on the case," Inspector Gong finally said as he pulled away slowly. He quickly righted his clothes as Lady Li smoother her chaopao.

"Oh?" she asked.

"It was a mistake to come here, to ask for your help," he said. "I haven't been able to think of anything else since I saw you again."

His words did not hurt her, because she knew he was right. There was something growing between them, something she was afraid to give a voice to, but if they continued giving into it, their lives would only be ruined.

Lady Li, her knees weak, fell ungraciously into her chair. "And now?" she asked. "What of the case?"

Inspector Gong remained standing, affecting an air of professionalism. "Can you get back into the legation? Find out more information?"

"What do you need to know?" she asked.

"We need to find her boyfriend," he said. "She was pregnant."

If Lady Li hadn't already been sitting she certainly would be now. "Pregnant? But she wasn't planning on leaving her position or marrying."

"So says everyone," Inspector Gong said. "Her mother knew about the boy, but she said they weren't planning on marrying. Her employer, Mrs. Gibson said the same thing. But if she were pregnant, that could ruin everything."

"Even if she wasn't planning on keeping it or marrying, if someone found out she was pregnant, she would be immediately dismissed and unable to find work in the legation again. Her reputation..." Lady Li stopped herself and shook her head. It didn't matter what a woman's class was, if she gave into her passions, she risked running her life.

"The missionaries would probably refuse to help her as well," Inspector Gong said.

Lady Li nodded. "Her parents would disown her."

"So why not just marry the boy?" he asked. "Seems like the safer and easier choice. He could at least keep his job. Why not tell him?"

"Maybe he wasn't the father," Lady Li said.

Inspector Gong nodded. "Yes, that was my suspicion as well. But would it matter? Just let the boy think it was his. Can you think of a reason why she wouldn't want him to think he was the father?"

"I can think of a few reasons," she said.

"A few?" Inspector Gong nearly choked out. "Damn, I couldn't think of one."

Lady Li suppressed a smile and shook her head. "I supposed men don't give much thought to these matters."

"It had never crossed my mind," Inspector Gong admitted. "So what do you think?"

"It is possible she and the boy had not slept together," she said. "How far along was she?"

"Three months," he said.

"That would be too far along to sleep with the boy and tell him the baby came early. No one would believe a baby was three months early. That only works after a month, six weeks at the most."

Inspector Gong was doing his best to keep his jaw from dropping. Lady Li wondered if he was thinking about all the times he heard about babies "coming early" and never thought anything of it. She tried not to laugh.

"And...your other...*revelations*?" he asked.

"She could be concerned the baby won't look like him," she said.

"I'm sure she could pass the baby off as looking like a distant relation," he said.

"A relation with yellow hair or green eyes?" she asked.

Again she watched as the gears in Inspector Gong's head whirled. "You think she could be pregnant with a yellow-haired child like Mr. Gibson?"

"It's possible," she said. "Even in Chinese households, it's not uncommon for men to take their maids to bed. In the Forbidden City, why do you think all the maids have to be Manchu? They have to be Manchu in case the Emperor decides to take them to his bed."

"You spoke to the Gibsons about the girl," he said. "Did they say anything to make you think there was something going on between the girl and Mr. Gibson?"

"No," she said, shaking her head. "Mrs. Gibson said she liked the girl very much."

"Any other reason why should wouldn't tell the boy?" he asked. "You said you had a few ideas."

"She might have been wanting to use the pregnancy to catch a better prize," she said. "Why pretend the baby belonged to a servant when she could pretend it belonged to someone with better prospects? But that is a very risky gamble."

Inspector Gong nodded. "Whatever path she chose was going to be risky."

"It was risky enough to cost her her life in the end," Lady Li said.

"We need to find the boyfriend," Inspector Gong said. "We need to find out what he knew and where he was the night of the murder."

"I can call on Lady Highcastle," Lady Li said. "She lives in one of the houses across from the Gibsons."

"Good," he said. "Start there and see what you can find out. According to the mother, the boy's name was Wang Bolin."

"If you know his name, can't you just go into the legation and ask them to hand him over?" Lady Li asked. "They probably won't stop you from arresting a Chinese."

"They might," he said. "They probably wouldn't take kindly to me barging in. And I don't know where he is. If I have to ask house by house, he could escape. No, I need to know where he is so I can move in quickly and capture him."

Lady Li nodded. "I will do my best to find him."

9

*T*he next day, the clothes Lady Li had ordered from a French tailor arrived.

"Oh, mistress," Concubine Swan said as she started pulling things out of the boxes. "Have you ever seen anything so fine?"

"You weren't with me in the Forbidden City," said Lady Li. "You wouldn't believe the hundreds of hours of embroidery work that must go into every single one of the empress's gowns."

"That must be a sight to see," Concubine Swan said as she tried to figure out which skirt went with which top and which hat.

"It certainly was," Lady Li said. "But these gowns are quite fine as well. The boning in the corsets is supposed to be the top quality."

"Oh, I don't know how you can even breathe in them," Concubine Swan said. "Every time you told the maid to tie the ties tighter I thought your ribs were going to snap."

"It is amazing what our bodies can endure in the name of fashion," Lady Li said with a smile.

"Surprising how strongly the foreign women are against foot binding when they bind their own bodies so," Concubine Swan said as she fiddled with the ties on Lady Li's new pair of walking boots.

Lady Li stood in front of her mirror as she tried on one of the hats. "It is a bit hypocritical. But the missionaries have prevented many young women from having to endure the practice, so whatever it takes."

"I don't know why the empress doesn't just outlaw the practice altogether," Concubine Swan said, giving up on trying to tie the laces on the boots.

"The empress has a tight road to walk," Lady Li said. "The Han grow more and more resentful of us Manchu every day. If she was to ban one of their more dear cultural practices, she could lose what little goodwill with the people she has."

"It is a terrible price those women have to pay," Concubine Swan lamented. "Our women are so lucky."

"Oh, I don't know," Lady Li said. "I don't know how many times I twisted my ankle on those dreadful pot-bottom shoes when I was younger."

"I suppose every culture has their own way of inflecting pain on us," Concubine Swan said.

"But we endure," Lady Li said. "We are stronger and smarter for it."

"Is that why Inspector Gong keeps coming by," Concubine Swan asked with a mischievous smile. "He can't seem to find his feet without you to help him."

Lady Li blushed. She certainly hoped that Concubine Swan didn't know about her...lack of decorum with Inspector Gong the day before. If anyone needed a man in her life, it was Concubine Swan. If Lady Li thought she could find a good placement for her, she would sell her. But she feared that anywhere she sent her, the poor girl would be even worse off than she was now. No respectable man would want a second-hand wife, especially one that had had a miscarriage.

"He just keeps getting assignments he is not able to investigate on his own," Lady Li said as she instructed her maid to help her put on one of the new outfits. "He doesn't speak English, and there is no way the foreigners will let him actually investigate them."

"Sounds like the prince needs to just hire women to work in his investigative force if his men can't get the job done," Concubine Swan said, sticking her chin out defiantly.

Lady Li started to laugh, but then she stopped herself. It wasn't a terrible idea. There were actually many places in Chinese society where men couldn't go. Men and women often led very separate lives. She was surprised the prince hadn't considered using women before she started working with Inspector Gong. And Lady Li shouldn't really be doing this sort of work. Maybe Concubine Swan could take her place. Of course, Lady Li would miss helping Inspector Gong with his cases, but it would be for the best.

"Would you like to come with me to call on Lady High-castle?" Lady Li asked Concubine Swan.

"What?" she asked, shocked. "Me? Go with you? Are you serious?"

Lady Li nodded. "Yes, I mean it. I'm sure the maid can tighten one of these dresses up to fit you." Concubine Swan was exceptionally thin, but she preferred eating opium to food. Lady Li hoped that helping with a case would give Concubine Swan something else to do.

"You'd let me wear one of your new French dresses?"

Concubine Swan asked, almost in tears. "Oh, mistress, you are too kind to me."

"Please, don't be emotional," Lady Li chided. "You know you are no mere slave, you are family. Now go clean yourself up and then come back and we will fit one of these gowns to you."

*C*oncubine Swan was nearly giddy as they were carried in the sedan chair to the legation to call on Lady Highcastle, both of their maids trotting along beside. When Lord Yun chose Concubine Swan, he also required that she be able to speak English as well. Not that he planned to use her as a spy the way he did his wife—he knew the foreigners would look down on him for having a concubine—but he would only accept a well-educated woman. And Lady Li supported him choosing someone from a similar background as herself. But since Concubine Swan entered the Yun household, she had very little use for her English, so she had forgotten quite a bit. So Lady Li spoke to her in English on the way to legation.

"Remember that your name is Yun Swan," Lady Li said. "And you are Lord Yun's cousin, not his concubine."

"I am Yun Swan," she said in English as she peeked out the curtain. "I am your cousin."

"Very good," Lady Li replied.

"I am so nervous," Concubine Swan said in Chinese. "I haven't left the house since I was brought there in a red chair."

Lady Li nodded. There were few opportunities for a married lady to leave her house after marriage. They could go to the temple on festival days, but Concubine Swan didn't seem to be very religious.

"You'll do fine," Lady Li said. "Just try to follow the conversation as best you can."

"Should I do anything to help with your investigation?" Concubine Swan asked. "Since that is the real reason why we are going."

"Don't do anything obvious," Lady Li said. "We don't want them to know we have anything to do with that. They won't trust us if they suspect we are just using them for information." Lady Li left out the fact that she actually enjoyed Mrs. Gibson's company and would like to renew their friendship.

When they arrived at the legation, once again, the ladies were allowed inside, but the men and the chair had to wait outside.

Lady Li felt much more confident this time, in her new frock in the latest fashion, but she couldn't ignore that the two of them together got even more stares than last time. She wasn't sure if it was because there were two of them or because of how stunning Concubine Swan looked. Concubine Swan was a beauty by any standard. She had a long, lean body, but in the corseted French gown, she suddenly had curves in all the womanly places. She had allowed her hair to fall freely around her shoulders, which accented her nearly white skin and dreamy doe eyes. Lady Li had never felt intimidated by Concubine Swan before, but the more she looked around at the people—the men—staring at them, she had to accept that they were staring at Concubine Swan.

Lady Li shrugged the bit of self-consciousness niggling at the back of her mind away. She needed to focus on the task at hand. She rang the bell at the home of Lady High-castle. A Chinese maid answered the door, her eyes wide at seeing two Chinese ladies in western dress standing there.

"Please let Lady Highcastle know that Lady Li is here to see her," Lady Li said in English. She could have said it in Chinese, but she wanted to make sure that the maid would actually deliver the message.

The maid gave a curt bow and headed inside. She returned a moment later and opened the door wide.

"Lady Highcastle will see you," she said in English. "Your maids can wait in the kitchen."

Lady Li nodded to the maids as she and Concubine Swan were led to the parlor. Lady Li started for a moment when she saw there were two other ladies already there with Lady Highcastle: Mrs. Gibson and another woman she didn't know.

"Lady Li!" Mrs Gibson called out as she crossed the room and took her hand. "How wonderful to see you again so soon. And what a lovely dress you are wearing."

"It is just an ugly dress the shop had in stock," Lady Li replied. "I thought that if I was going to resume my visits in the legation, I should update my wardrobe."

"Well I think you look lovely," Mrs. Gibson said. "And who is your friend?"

"This is my cousin," Lady Li said. "My late husband's cousin actually. She is practicing her English and wanted to accompany me."

"I am Swan," Concubine Swan said slowly and clearly,

gripping Mrs. Gibson's hand and shaking it vigorously. "I am her cousin."

"Charmed," Mrs. Gibson said. "Well, come over and sit down. Lady Li, I am sure you recall Lady Highcastle."

"Just who I was coming to visit," Lady Li said as she approached a younger woman with soft brown curls. "I am so sorry to have called when you already have visitors."

"Not at all," Lady Highcastle said. "I appreciate having company. This...sordid business has been terrible for my nerves. Do sit down and have some tea."

Lady Li sat down on a small couch, and Concubine Swan sat next to her. Another Chinese maid who had been standing nearby offered each of them a teacup and poured the tea for them. Lady Li noticed that Concubine Swan gripped the delicate British-style cup firmly in both of her hands. She hadn't considered giving the girl a rundown of British manners. She nudged Concubine Swan with her elbow and held up her own teacup, gently held by and handle with her fingers. Concubine Swan nodded and followed her example.

"Lady Li," Lady Highcastle said, "do you know Mrs. Belvedere?"

Lady Li recalled that Mrs. Belvedere lived in the other house across from the Gibsons. "I'm afraid I do not," she said. "You must be new to Peking."

Mrs. Belvedere was older and had a face like a sour plum. "I have been here for two years," she said. "But one never feels settled in a foreign country. Every single day is a struggle. Do you know I spent two hours at the bank yesterday trying to send money home? Two hours! The whole day was practically shot by the time I got back to the legation."

All the ladies nodded and then sipped their tea.

"And you can never find good help," Mrs. Belvedere continued. "None of the servants could catch up with their work when I got home. We were not served dinner until nine o'clock! I have never lived in a country with such lazy people. And we lived in India for a decade!"

Lady Li did not reply but kept to her tea.

"What is India?" Concubine Swan asked.

"*Yìndù*," Lady Li said softly.

"Oh yes," Concubine Swan said with a smile and nod.

"Have you been to India?" Lady Highcastle asked Concubine Swan.

Concubine Swan giggled. "No. I just know the name. Tea and opium, yes?"

The other women laughed uncomfortably.

"I am sure India has more than that to offer," Mrs. Gibson said.

"But that is about it in a nutshell," Lady Highcastle said.

"And malaria," Mrs. Belvedere said. "And the heat. And the humidity! And the smell! Oh, my lord. If I never smell..."

"When will you return to England, Mrs. Belvedere?" Lady Li asked in the hopes of redirecting the conversation.

"Heaven knows!" she replied, throwing up her hands. "Have you heard about the ports being closed? We were supposed to leave next month so we can be home for Christmas. I tell you, that Mr. Hart is ruining lives as we speak. Not only was my husband's ship locked in the port for some dreadful inspection, even passenger ships have been prevented from leaving."

"How terribly inconvenient," Lady Li said innocently.

"We were lucky that my husband's captain was anxious to leave and left early," Mrs. Gibson said.

"Well some of us weren't," Mrs. Belvedere said. "Our silk

and porcelain goods were scheduled to ship next week, but Mr. Hart said that the inspection could last a month!"

"Not to mention the ships that now can't get in," Lady Highcastle said. "Most of our husbands import as well."

"Indeed," Mrs. Gibson said. "Our ship got out but our next arrival has been delayed indefinitely. I don't know what Hart expects them to do. Just float around in circles for weeks on end? What about our letters from home?"

"It's an act of war, I tell you!" Mrs. Belvedere exclaimed rather suddenly, causing Lady Li to nearly spit out her tea.

"Oh, Julia," Lady Highcastle said, patting Mrs. Belvedere's hand. "It can't be a bad as that, can it?"

"It certainly is!" Mrs. Belvedere said. "We were awarded those trade ports fair and square after the last war. To close them is to violate the peace treaty."

Lady Li could feel her left eye twitch and her cheeks burn. She knew she needed to keep silent if she wished to gain information from the ladies, but as she bit the inside of her cheek to the point of bleeding, she simply could not.

"I am sure that any losses will pale in comparison to the losses the Chinese suffered during the war," she said. "The emperor died because of it. I am sure a few days' delay of a ship is only a minor inconvenience."

The other ladies were silent for a moment as the tension mounted. The other ladies shuffled uncomfortably as Lady Li locked eyes with Mrs. Belvedere.

"I would not expect you to understand matters of economic importance," Mrs. Belvedere finally said to Lady Li. "Chinese women aren't even allowed to go to school, much less be educated in such complex matters."

"And considering how young England is when compared to China," Lady Li said, "I can understand why your people have such little regard for the culture, the traditions, the architecture of the people you conquer."

"Architecture?" Mrs. Belvedere scoffed. "You mean those ridiculous squat houses and open-air temples? It's just wood and paint. Nothing of substance like the great marble structures we build. We did China a favor by burning down that wretched Summer 'Palace' as the locals like to call it."

"Did you see the Summer Palace before your people came?" Lady Li asked.

"Of course, not," Mrs. Belvedere said.

"I did," Lady Li said. "I was there when it burned. I watched from a nearby cliff as hundreds of buildings, countless of pieces of art, and thousands of years of history went up in smoke. After your soldiers looted what they could like common thieves."

"Oh, Lady Li," Lady Highcastle said, her hand on her chest. "How terrible that much have been for you."

"Well," Mrs. Belvedere huffed. "You would think that you people would have learned your lesson. Defying the will of the British will only cost you *dearly*."

"Did you learn your lesson after the American Revolution?" Lady Li asked. "Great Britain can only force its will upon the world for so long."

Mrs. Belvedere stood. "Well, I think I have had quite enough tea. Good day to you all."

The other ladies all stood. Lady Highcastle tried to see Mrs. Belvedere out, but she nearly rushed out without even a goodbye.

"Perhaps we should go as well," Lady Li said. "I fear I let my stupid tongue say too much."

"Oh no," Mrs. Gibson said, sitting back down. "Do stay. Mrs. Belvedere is always a negative Nelly."

"She is a hard woman to get to know," Lady Highcastle said as she sat.

"Lady Highcastle," Concubine Swan said very formally. "How are you coping after the murder?"

Lady Li gasped. "Con...Cousin Swan! How can you ask such a thing? I am so sorry, ladies."

Lady Highcastle and Mrs. Gibson looked at each other and then burst out laughing.

"It's quite all right, Lady Li," Lady Highcastle said. "Do you think we have talked about anything else since that day?"

"It has been quite stressful, in truth," Lady Highcastle replied. "That there is a murderer running loose in the legation, it is terrifying. She was shot from outside! We aren't even safe in our own homes."

"I have heard that the police are looking for the young woman's boyfriend," Lady Li said. "Someone name Wang Bolin."

"Wang Bolin?" Lady Highcastle asked. "Are you serious? Where did you hear that?"

She stammered for a moment, unsure of how to reply. How would she hear something so specific?

"The Chinese newspaper," Concubine Swan said.

Lady Li looked at her in shock, but she only nodded for Lady Li to go along.

"Oh, yes, the Chinese newspaper," Lady Li said. "I am sure the Chinese newspapers and the English newspapers are each printing their own versions of what happened."

Lady Highcastle and Mrs. Belvedere nodded, accepting the explanation.

"Do they think he did it?" Lady Highcastle asked.

"I think it is just routine to question anyone who was close to the girl," Lady Li said.

"Well, Mrs. Belvedere is going to love that," Lady Highcastle said. "Wang Bolin is a member of her staff."

"Oh." Lady Li nearly shuddered. It would be impossible for her to speak with Mrs. Belvedere after their last exchange. What would Inspector Gong think? "Are you sure?"

"Quite sure," Lady Highcastle said. "I remember because she was concerned he would be leaving to get married. And it is so hard to find male Chinese servants who speak English. Chinese women who speak English are difficult enough to find, but a man is like finding the Holy Grail."

"Oh, you are right," Mrs. Gibson said. "I remember that now. It didn't dawn on me when she was telling us about it that he was the young man who had been courting Weilin. It makes perfect sense now."

Lady Li sipped at her tea, which had long gone cold and pondered how she was going to break this news to Inspector Gong. He was certainly going to be unhappy with the fact that she had made an enemy of the woman who could keep him from taking Wang into custody.

A clock on the mantle chimed.

"Will you look at the time," Lady Highcastle said. "I am sorry but my children will be home from school soon."

The ladies all stood.

"Not at all," Lady Li said. "I do hope I may visit again."

"Of course," Lady Highcastle said. "I do enjoy having someone with...a different point of view in the room."

They all said their goodbyes, and then Lady Li and Concubine Swan made their way back to the front gate of the legation. As soon as they got into their sedan chair, Concubine Swan began laughing hysterically.

"That was wonderful," she said in Chinese.

"It was dreadful!" Lady Li replied. "Mrs. Belvedere is going to have me banned from legation forever!"

"No," Concubine Swan said. "The other ladies won't let her. They hate her."

"What do you mean?" Lady Li asked.

'The way they look at her, talk to her. The young lady, she defended you," Concubine Swan said. "No, I think they do not like that wrinkled old sow."

"Watch your tongue!" Lady Li said harshly. "And what was that? 'What do you think about the murder?' How could you be so blunt?"

Concubine Swan waved her concerns away. "You were taking too long. You were never going to learn anything."

"Please," Lady Li begged. "You must be more cautious."

"Fine," Concubine Swan said. "Next time I will be more discreet."

"You think there will be a next time?" Lady Li asked.

"Oh please, my lady!" Concubine Swan cried as she pulled on Lady Li's hand. "Let me help you. Do not lock me up at home! It is so boring there."

Lady Li sighed. "I don't keep you captive. You know this is our life, to be in the house and never to leave."

"But you found a way to leave," Concubine Swan said. "By helping the inspector and making friends with foreign ladies. Please don't leave me behind."

Lady Li patted the girl's hand. "I will see what I can do," she said. "But I make no promises."

*a*s Inspector Gong and Prince Kung neared the legation, a crowed formed behind them. The people knew that the prince would not be heading to the legation unless there had been a development.

"We have to act fast," Inspector Gong said. "Get in, grab the boy, grab his belongings, and get out."

"If we can get into the house at all," the prince grumbled. "This is going to be a nightmare."

"He will hear us coming," the inspector said. "As soon as we get inside the gate, word will spread faster than we can walk. He will try to escape. We will station our men around the wall, but we need to keep our eyes open."

The prince nodded and jumped out of the chair as soon as it stopped outside the legation. He marched up to the gate, which was immediately opened for him and his men. But as they all walked toward the British quarter, the British police chief and consuls rushed forward. Prince Kung did not stop as he explained his haste to them. If he stopped to explain, the boy would run.

But the prince, the inspector, and their men could only get so far. When they arrived at the Belvedere's house, a large man and an angry woman came out and stood on the porch.

The man barked angry words at the prince that Inspector Gong did not understand. Prince Kung nodded and did his best to explain the situation, but Inspector Gong did not hold out hope that they would be allowed inside the house. He stood back so he could watch the front and left side of the house. He looked at the windows up above where he could see servants peeking out. All along the street, Chinese and foreigners were gathering.

Suddenly, Inspector Gong heard someone call out, "Watch out!" in Chinese. He looked down the road and saw a young man with a bulky coat and large satchel collide with a maid who had been carrying a box of oranges. The oranges spilled onto the street, causing the young man to stumble and struggle to get back to his feet.

"Hey! Stop!" the inspector called out. The young man looked back at him, but then turned away and ran. Inspector Gong ran after him. The young man was fast, but he was bogged down by his clothes and his bag. When he saw that Inspector Gong was catching up with him, he dropped his bag, but there was nothing he could do about his clothes. He had only made it the length of three or four houses when Inspector Gong leaped on him, dragging him to the ground.

Inspector Gong grabbed the boy by his shirt. "Are you Wang Bolin?" he asked. The boy did not respond, so Inspector Gong punched him in the face. "Are you Wang Bolin?" he shouted again.

"Yes! Yes!" the boy cried.

"Get up," the inspector ordered as he dragged Wang to his feet.

The prince and several of the prince's men ran up the inspector.

"Don't talk to anyone on your way out or they might try to stop you," the prince said.

The inspector nodded.

"We cannot get inside the house," the prince said. "It is impossible."

"Don't worry," the inspector said. As they approached the bag that Wang had dropped, he reached down and picked it up. "Everything the boy owns is probably in this bag."

Several foreign men did approach the inspector and the prince. The inspector ignored them all, but the prince did reply to some of them as he kept on walking. The foreigners seemed irritated that the inspector was making an arrest in the legation, but they did not want to physically stop him and risk angering the prince.

As they approached the gate, the inspector worried for a moment that it would not open for them, but it did. However, he was not prepared to meet the crowds outside.

Hundreds of people had gathered, and when they saw that Inspector Gong was dragging a Chinese man out of the legation with a bloody nose, the crowd erupted into shouts and jeers. They pushed in toward the gate, and the prince's men had to forcedly push their way through the crowd so that the prince and the inspector could take their captive to their sedan chair.

"Is that him?" a voice called out from behind the inspector. "Is that the man who killed my girl?"

The crowd yelled louder.

The inspector threw the young man into the sedan chair and then turned to the dead girl's father. "I don't know anything yet," the inspector said. "I just want to question him."

"Is this the boy who was trying to seduce her?" he pressed.

"I don't know," the inspector said as he got into the chair. "I will be in contact with you soon. You need to leave this place." He motioned to the crowd. "No good will come of this."

"You get justice your way, inspector," the father said. "And I will get it in mine."

Inspector Gong didn't like the sound of those words, but he couldn't wait around to see what would happen. He instructed his men to try to disperse the crowd as best they could without resorting to violence. But he had no faith they would succeed.

*I*nspector Gong took the young man to the Ministry of Justice, a dungeon below the Forbidden City. He dragged the boy out of the sedan chair and down the stairs into the dark and winding paths of the Ministry of Justice. Prince Gong did not accompany the inspector—he trusted him to get the information they needed.

The inspector took the boy to a small room and tossed him inside. He closed the door behind them.

"Please, please," the young man, who could not have been more than twenty, sniveled.

"Please what?" the inspector asked.

"Please don't kill me," the boy said.

"Why would I kill you?" the inspector asked as he tossed the boy to the floor. The room had no windows and no other doors. There was a pile of moldy straw in one corner and a hole in the floor where a person could piss. The room was dark, dank, and terrifying.

"Because you think I killed Weilin," he said.

"Did you?" the inspector asked.

"I couldn't!" the boy cried as he got to his knees and kowtowed before the inspector. "I love her! I wanted to marry her!"

"Then why didn't you?" the inspector asked.

"She wanted to wait," the boy said. "She has to support her family. She makes good money in the legation."

The inspector noticed that the boy spoke in the present tense, as if the girl were still alive. That was something murderers didn't usually do.

"So what is in your bag?" the inspector asked, picking up the rucksack and opening it.

"No!" Wang yelled, reaching for it.

Inspector Gong placed his foot on Wang's chest and pushed him back. "Stay down there!" He opened the bag and pulled out some extra clothes, a couple of books, and some food. As one of the shirts unrolled, something clattered to the floor.

It was the arrow the inspector had last seen in the girl's chest.

The inspector looked at Wang, and the two locked eyes.

The boy scrambled away, as if he would try to run, but there was nowhere to go. Inspector Gong picked up the arrow, then he grabbed Wang's shirt and tossed him into a wall.

"Where did you get this?" Inspector Gong demanded. "Why do you have it?"

"I just wanted it to remember her by," the boy said. "They put her body in a box in the Gibsons' basement. I crawled in through a window. I just wanted to see her one last time! The arrow was in the box. I took it. I didn't think! I just miss her so much!"

"Are you an idiot?" Inspector Gong asked as the boy started to cry again. "Or are you trying to steal evidence? Where did you really get it? Why would you kill her with something so ornate?"

"I didn't," he screamed. "I didn't! It wasn't mine. Her father made it. It must have been a gift for her or something."

"Her father made it?" Inspector Gong asked, loosening his grip.

"He's a woodcarver. Old family trade," the boy said, calming slightly.

Inspector Gong remembered that the old man had told him that he was a woodcarver. He said he made door carvings, but it would make sense he could make any kind of woodcarving. But why would the old man give her the arrow? Would he have killed her with it? If he thought she had dishonored the family in some way, he could have thought he was justified. In many ways, he would be. Family disputes often resulted in deaths, and if the dead person was the property of the killer, a child or a concubine, the killer often faced no consequences. If the old man had killed the girl in his own home instead of in the legation, no one would have batted an eye.

But if the old man had killed her, that would mean he somehow got into the legation, climbed to the roof of the Belvedere house, and then waited for the perfect moment to kill the girl when she was in a room that wasn't her own.

No, it was too farfetched. It didn't make any sense.

However, the father could have hired someone, like Wang, to kill the girl. But if Wang loved her, he wouldn't have killed her. Unless he had his own reason to.

"You said the girl wouldn't marry you," Inspector Gong said. "Did that make you angry?"

"No," Wang said. "Not really. Disappointed, maybe. But life for legation Chinese is different. Outside the legation, she was already very old to not be married. But for us who work in legation, the money is very good, and the employment can last many years. It is common for girls to wait, especially if the family needs the money."

"She wouldn't get married even if she was pregnant?" Inspector Gong asked.

Wang looked up at him with confusion on his face. Inspector Gong waited for what he said to sink in.

"Weilin..." he started to say. "She was not...she could not be with a child."

"Why not?"

The boy grew red-faced. "We...she did not want to...we didn't..."

"You didn't have sex with her?" Inspector Gong asked plainly.

Wang lowered his head and shook it.

"Why not?" Inspector Gong asked. "Don't you know how?"

"Of course I do!" Wang yelled. "But she said she couldn't risk it. All the girls, if they get pregnant, they get kicked out."

"But Weilin was pregnant," Inspector Gong said. "Who was the father if it wasn't you?"

Wang dropped his head again and started to cry. "How could she? I don't know! I love her. I was good to her. We wanted a future, a family. Here!" He pulled open his shirt. He was wearing another one underneath, and another one.

"Why are you wearing so much?" Inspector Gong asked him.

"Less to carry this way," Wang admitted. "I was ready to run before you showed up. I knew you would come for me since she was my girl." He rummaged around in his shirts, and then in his many layers of pants and pulled out a bunch of folded pieces of paper. "Letters from Weilin to me. You will see that we loved each other. I wouldn't do this. And she wouldn't be a whore."

Inspector took the letters and opened one of them. They were written in English.

"Why are they written in English?" Inspector Gong asked.

"To protect her," Wang explained. "Her parents cannot read English. So this way, if someone found them and tried to tell her parents, they would not know what they said."

"Is this all of them?" Inspector Gong asked. "I want them all."

The inspector helped Wang find all the letters hidden about his person. There were dozens. He looked at the letters and pretended he knew what they said, but he would have to ask Lady Li to translate them.

"I'm going to take all of these and read them," Inspector Gong said. "And then I'm going to come back and question you some more."

"I hope you do," Wang said. "I love her. I want to know who hurt her."

"As do I," Inspector Gong said. He took the letters and the arrow and left the room, shutting Wang in darkness with only the rats for company.

11

"*E*unuch Bai!" Lady Li called from her desk where she was working on the household accounts. He did not respond. "Eunuch Bai!" she called again. Again, he did not respond. "Where is that man?" she grumbled to herself as she put away her pen and nearly stomped across the room.

As she opened the door to her office, she saw a maid walking by. "Where is Eunuch Bai?" she asked the maid.

"I don't know, my lady," the maid replied with her head down. "Should I check the kitchens?"

"Yes," Lady Li said. "And where are my daughters?"

"I saw them in the courtyard with their grandmother," the maid said. "Should I fetch them for you?"

"No," Lady Li said. "I'll get them."

Lady Li went to the courtyard where she saw Popo sitting in a chair in the sun while her youngest daughter was playing with some flowers.

"Where is First Daughter?" Lady Li asked.

Popo motioned across the yard. "Peeking at the street," she said.

"Why are you letting her?" Lady Li asked, exasperated. "Does no one follow the rules around here?"

She walked across the yard and saw her eldest daughter standing on a crate by the wall, peeking through the small decorative cutouts to the street.

"Daughter!" Lady Li called. "Come here this instant."

The girl immediately jumped down and ran to her mother. "I'm sorry, mother," she said. "But there are so many people outside. What is happening?"

"What?" Lady Li asked. "Where is Eunuch Bai? He would know."

"I haven't seen him today," her daughter said.

Lady Li huffed and walked to the wall, peering through a small window herself. There were many people outside, more than on the day of the girl's murder, and they were heading toward the legation.

"Death to the White Devils!" she heard someone call.

"Down with the Qing!" another said.

"Make China strong!" others yelled.

Lady Li stepped back and felt her heart racing. This was bad. She wasn't sure what was causing the people to be upset, but she was beginning to feel afraid. Han nationalism had been gaining ground ever since the last war with the foreigners. Any rebellions against foreigners often spilled over into rebellions against the Manchu as well. Many people considered the Manchu to be just as foreign as the British or Germans were. And in some ways, they were.

The Manchu had invaded China over three hundred years ago. Traditionally, Manchu people were from the steppes north of China and had never been subjected to the Chinese emperors. But when the Manchu saw how weak the Ming had become, they seized their chance and invaded. Emperor Hong Taiji founded the Qing Dynasty and created a two-class system: the Manchu, and everyone else. The Manchu set themselves apart from the Han Chinese people. The Manchu imposed their traditions on the Chinese, such as how they dressed or how local governments were run, but the Han and the Manchu were still very separate people.

The Han Chinese, though, outnumbered the Manchu ten-to-one. It would only be a matter of time before China returned to the Chinese. Every Manchu knew this and feared when that day would come. Every small rebellion was dealt with quickly and severely. Yet the anti-Manchu sentiment continued to grow.

Lady Li stepped away from the wall and grabbed her daughter's hand as she walked back to Popo.

"Stay away from the wall, do you understand me?" Lady Li ordered.

"Yes, mama," her daughter said as she sat next to her sister.

Lady Li sat in a chair next to Popo. "Where is Eunuch Bai?" she asked her.

"I don't know," Popo said. "He has been quiet for several days. Something is bothering him."

Lady Li had noticed, and she knew why. Of course, he knew what Lady Li had done with Inspector Gong. After the inspector left that day, Eunuch Bai had not made eye contact with Lady Li or spoken to her directly, and she had been too ashamed to speak to him about anything other than the most necessary of topics.

She had been foolish, reckless. Stupid. She would not be surprised if Eunuch Bai had simply abandoned her. If she ruined her life, there was no sense in him going down with her.

"What will happen?" Popo asked. "If you don't find out who killed that girl?"

Lady Li shook her head. "I don't know. Something very terrible could happen. Or it could amount to nothing at all."

"You, me, Concubine Swan," Popo said. "Three women, trapped and alone. Should things go badly, we have nowhere to go."

"Where is Concubine Swan?" Lady Li asked.

Popo glanced toward Concubine Swan's quarters, but said nothing. Lady Li took it as silent confirmation that she was in her room in an opium cloud. She sighed and decided to worry about that later.

"The empress would always take us in," Lady Li said.

"Did that keep you safe last time?" Popo asked.

Lady Li shuddered at the memory of having to flee the Summer Palace in the middle of the night.

"We need someone to protect us," Popo said.

"What are you saying?" Lady Li asked. "What do you expect me to do?"

"You need to marry," Popo said plainly. Lady Li scoffed, but Popo held up her hand. "We need an ally. Someone with a house with stronger walls, or a home outside the city. Or someone with a ship."

Lady Li's eyes grew big. "Are you saying we should... leave China?"

"Not now," Popo said. "But dark days are coming, my girl, and we need protection."

"You know I can't marry," Lady Li said. "What about the girls? What about my reputation?"

"Your first obligation to the girls is to keep them safe, not keep them rich," Popo said.

"But still," Lady Li said. "I can't simply marry someone.

The empress would have to approve, and he would have to be of high enough standing..."

"Than ask her," Popo said. "Ask the empress to find you a husband. I am sure that if the prince would still have you..."

"Oh, Popo," Lady Li said. "How can you suggest such a thing? You know we were nearly engaged before. Besides, if you want to keep us safe, I don't think linking us closer to the imperial family is the answer."

"Then perhaps as far from the imperial family as possible?" Popo asked. "Like that inspector."

Lady Li snorted a laugh. "You would have me marry a Han? Now I know you have lost your faculties."

"We are too vulnerable, my girl," Popo said. "You must..."

"What I must do," Lady Li said, "is make sure the land in tilled in the spring and the pigs are brought to market on time. So if you will excuse me, I need to find Eunuch Bai."

Lady Li stood and returned to her study. She could not believe what Popo had just suggested to her. She couldn't marry. She wouldn't! She had gone over this a hundred times in her own head. A thousand times! It was why she had taken Inspector Gong as a one-time...two-time lover. He helped her feel human again, helped her feel alive, but that was all. She couldn't marry, couldn't risk everything she had. Her daughters' future.

Why did she feel like everything was closing in around her? Like she would have to soon make a choice, and that it would be the wrong one?

"Mistress?" A maid knocked on her door.

"Yes?" Lady Li asked. "Did you find Eunuch Bai?"

"No, mistress," the maid replied. "But Inspector Gong is here to see you."

"You must be joking," Lady Li replied, rubbing her temple.

"Should I send him in?" the maid asked.

"Yes," Lady Li replied, "but leave the door open."

"Yes, mistress," the maid replied. She was gone but a minute when she returned with Inspector Gong behind her. The maid bowed and then left the room.

The inspector smiled when he saw Lady Li, but he took note of the open door. He looked at Lady Li, but she made no move to close the door.

"Please, have a seat," she said as she moved to a chair.

"Thank you, Lady Li," he said.

"Do you have any news?" she asked. "What is happening outside? There are so many angry people."

"Hasn't Eunuch Bai kept you informed?" he asked.

"Unfortunately, Eunuch Bai and I are not exactly on speaking terms," she said.

He gave her a knowing nod. "I am sorry for that," he said sincerely.

She waved him away. "It's not your fault. But tell me, what is going on?"

"We found Wang Bolin," he said. "We arrested him, so of course the Chinese were not happy."

"Naturally," Lady Li said. "Has he confessed?"

"Quite the contrary," he said. "He insists that they were in love and he would never hurt her."

"Did you tell him about the baby?" Lady Li asked.

"I did," he said. "He said it wasn't his. That they had not been together. He says that she and most of the legation girls don't do such things because a pregnancy would cost them their jobs."

"And you believe him?" she asked.

"I think so," he said. "He seemed sincere. But he also

gave me these." He reached into his robe and pulled out a small packet of letters. "He said these are love letters she sent him. But they are in English, so I can't read them." He handed her the packet.

Lady Li untied the stack and looked at them. They were in English, but translating hand-written English to Chinese was not something she had much practice with.

"Forgive me," she said. "But her handwriting is quite small. It will be difficult for me to read."

"Take your time," he said. "Should I come back?"

"No," she said. "Just give me a few minutes. Please have some tea."

He smiled and nodded as he sipped the tea, and her heart skipped. She willed it to stop. She could not have sentimental feelings for this man. She focused on the letters.

They were love letters. She used words like darling, dearest, and my love throughout. She also spoke of marriage, but in distant terms.

"She does say that she looked forward to being his wife," Lady Li explained. "But in English, that is an uncertain time. Far in the future."

She spoke of her parents, and how they were unhappy that she would not be home for Chinese New Year.

"It looks like the families of the legation do not let their Chinese employees celebrate Chinese holidays," she says. "They must work for Spring Festival. She had to work for Mid-Autumn Festival as well."

Inspector Gong scoffed. "Do they allow their British servants to celebrate Christmas?" he asked.

"She doesn't say," Lady Li said. "But I assume so."

One letter, though, seemed to take a darker turn.

"She says here that she doesn't have much time, and

that she can't help but worry. She says, 'if he comes back, I don't know how I will survive'."

"That sounds rather serious," Inspector Gong said, leaning forward. "Does she say who she is afraid of."

"No," Lady Li said, rereading the letter. "No names, and I can't tell from the context who she is speaking of."

"But Wang must have known," he said. "He must have known who she was referencing."

"You will have to ask him about that," she said.

"Can you underline that?" Inspector Gong asked. "And write it in Chinese so I can point it out to him later?"

"Yes, of course," Lady Li said, moving to her desk and her writing instruments.

"Anything else?" he asked.

Lady Li nodded. "She mentions being late to work one morning because she had to send money to someone."

"Her parents?" Inspector Gong asked.

"I don't think so," Lady Li said. "Oh, this one has a name. 'I was late to work because I sent the last of my money to Jiaolong. My mistress was furious'."

"So who is Jiaolong?" Inspector Gong asked.

"Another question for Wang, I suppose," Lady Li said.

"Or her parents," he said. "If she was sending money to him and not them, they must have known about it."

"Maybe he is the father," Lady Li said.

"If he is, then I am surprised she mentioned it in a letter to Wang," he said. "Mark that name too."

"Of course," she said. "I'm sorry I can't be of more help. I think you only have more questions to ask." She handed him back the letters.

"This is how it goes," he said. "Ask more and more questions until I get the right answer. You were a great help."

She smiled at him, and then blushed and turned away. "It was nothing," she said.

He took her hand and pulled her from her chair.

"Please don't," she said as she ripped her hand from his grasp and stepped away. "I can't...We can't...You should go."

The inspector looked to the open door and pressed his lips into a fine line. "I understand," he said curtly. "Thank you for your assistance."

He left the room and slammed the door behind him.

Lady Li sank back into her seat and would not allow herself to cry.

She had done the right thing in sending him away so coldly. Hadn't she?

12

*I*nspector Gong left Lady Li's in a huff. He wasn't sure why. After all, she had the right to reject him in her own home. She had left the door to her office open as a clear message that she did not want anything personal to happen between them. Yet, her refusal of even his touch hurt. She told him that she wanted him the other day when he took her in her sitting room. She clearly enjoyed it. So why was she being so cold to him now?

Perhaps she was regretting it. Maybe she felt guilty. What if they had been caught? Eunuch Bai certainly knew what happened. What if he had threatened to reveal her? If anyone was threatening her, even her dear eunuch, he would kill whoever it was. Maybe he should go back and tell her that he would protect her, no matter what.

Going to her house twice in one day, and now so late, would not look good. Perhaps he should just send her a note. Would she receive it, though? Eunuch Bai most likely accepted all of the household's correspondence.

He ran his hand over his forehead in frustration. He had let his emotions get the better of him. He stomped out when he should have stayed. He abandoned her when he should have stood by her side.

He felt trapped. He couldn't go back now, but he hated that he had to leave her alone. He didn't know what to do.

It was also too late to locate the Zhao family or go to the Ministry of Justice to interrogate Wang further. He went home. If he rested, perhaps things would be more clear.

When he got home, the family complex was quiet. Since it was autumn, the evenings in Peking were quite cool, so the family did not congregate in the courtyard like usual. But he could see lights and hear laughter and chatter from several of the living quarters. He did not visit with any of them though. He went to his own room and ordered some baijiu and dumplings from a maid. When the maid returned with his food, he considered ordering her to stay with him, but then thought better of it.

He had barely eaten a bite when he heard a knock on his door.

"Enter," he said. He was surprised when his mother walked in.

"You slipped in like a ghost," she said. "Are you avoiding me?"

"No," he said. "Just tired. This case is weighing on my mind."

"Can I help you with it?" she asked.

"I don't think so," he said. "You are kind to offer, but I have more than enough help."

"Well, maybe when you solve this case, you can take a break to focus on more important things," she said.

"Like what?" he asked as he sipped his baijiu.

"Like family," she hedged. He didn't say anything, but waited for her to continue. "Like...starting your own family," she finally finished.

"Don't think you are being sneaky," Inspector Gong said. "I find out information about people for a living. I know that you've been making inquiries."

"And you are not angry?" she asked, a gleam of hope in her eye.

He sighed. "I don't know how I feel about it," he said.

"That's good!" his mother said with a bit too much excitement. The fact that he wasn't thoroughly rejecting her mention of marriage was an improvement to her. "You have been so different lately. So much more...mature. Settled. Yet...unsettled. You are looking for something more in life, aren't you?"

He nodded. "Perhaps," he said. "But I don't know that a wife is the answer." In fact, he knew it wasn't. Well, not just any wife. He wanted Lady Li, but he knew even the force of nature that was his mother couldn't make that happen.

"You know how this works," she said. "If you give me your blessing to make a marriage inquiry, and your father and I arrange a match, there is no going back. You can't reject her if you change your mind later. Once the deal is struck, the girl we choose will be your wife, even before the ceremony."

"I know," he said. "Which is why I'm not saying yes just yet. I want to see her first."

His mother gasped. "You know you can't do that. It would be too...personal, too intimate to see her before the wedding."

"Paint a picture if you must," he said. "I won't marry a girl I've never seen."

She sighed. "I'll see what I can do."

"She also needs to be smart," he said. "Not just a dumb girl who can sit at my feet and wait for me to talk. She needs to be able to hold a conversation."

"By the Gods!" his mother exclaimed. "Whoever asked for such a thing in a wife? No one! Why do you need to talk to her? She just needs to lay on her back and make sons."

"That's exactly what I don't want," he said. "Is that all you do for Baba?"

His mother leaned over and moved to strike him, but he jerked out of the way.

"Where did I get such a vulgar, ungrateful child?" she asked.

"Smart," he said. "And pretty."

"Any other ridiculous requirements?" she asked.

He paused for a moment, because he knew the next request would be the one to send her over the edge.

"And...she can't have bound feet."

"What?" his mother nearly screamed. "What do you want? A dirty peasant girl to be my daughter-in-law? You have been spending too much time with that Manchu prince! He spits on our people and our ways. He will let the foreigners run right over our people in the streets."

"Mama!" Inspector Gong said firmly. "Don't speak about Prince Kung that way. You know he has done much for me and this family. He only does what is best for China. For *all* Chinese."

His mother stood up to leave the room. "If you don't want a wife why didn't you just say so?" she asked.

"I will honor my words," he said. "If you want me to marry, she needs to be pretty, smart, and flat-footed. It is up to you if you want another daughter-in-law or not."

"You are a cruel child," she said.

As she left, he almost laughed to himself. She was so mad. But then the reality of his situation sat in the depths of his stomach like a stone.

This was his mother he was talking about. If she set her mind to something, she accomplished it.

He was going to be married.

The next morning, Inspector Gong woke with a throbbing headache. At first, he couldn't remember what happened. But as he dressed, he kicked the empty bottle of baijiu and clarity hit him like a lightning bolt. He threw on his clothes and rushed to the family's communal dining area. Two of his sisters and one of his older brothers were sitting there eating their breakfast.

"You look like shit," his sister Biyu said as she put a dumpling in her mouth.

"Shut up," he said harshly. "Where is mother?"

"She's out," his other sister Daiyu said. "She knew as soon as you woke up you would change your mind, so she left at first light to make inquiries for a bride."

"Damnit!" he said.

"It's about time, brother," his brother Zhuang said as he offered Inspector Gong a bowl of congee. "But must you insult us all by marrying a flat-footed girl?"

"I'm not marrying anyone," he said as he waved away the offered bowl. "I have work to do. But when mother comes back, tell her not to make any deals!"

"You know it's too late," Daiyu teased, waving her chopsticks at him. "You'll be married by sundown."

He stomped away as his siblings laughed in the background.

What had he done? How was he going to tell Lady Li?

He had screwed up, and not for the first time in his life. But he needed to get his head out of his ass and focus on his case. He was running late, and his men were already waiting outside his house for their orders. He had two of them accompany him and told the others to await further instructions.

As he passed by the foreign legation on the way to the neighborhood where the dead girl's parents lived, he noticed that the crowd outside was even bigger than before. They weren't rioting, but it was only a matter of time.

As he approached the Zhaos' house, neighbors who had been sitting or working outside scattered. He knew he did not have a friendly bearing. He was walking quickly, and was followed by two of his biggest men. When he arrived at the house, the door was open to let in the morning sun.

"Zhao Laoye. Zhao Fuwen," he called as he stepped inside. "We need to talk."

They both came out of a side room. "What is all this?" Mr. Zhao asked.

"Sit," Inspector Gong ordered as he sat at one side of a table. "We need to talk about your daughter."

They both sat down uneasily.

"What have you found out?" Mr. Zhao asked.

Inspector Gong reached into his bag and pulled out the arrow. As he laid it on the table, Mrs. Zhao gasped and began to cry.

"What is this?" Mr. Zhao asked as he recoiled from the arrow like a snake.

"This is the weapon that was used to kill your daughter," Inspector Gong said. "You are a woodcarver, yes?"

Mr. Zhao pressed his lips, then slowly nodded.

"Did you make this arrow?" the inspector asked.

He shook his head. "It is an old family heirloom," the man said. "It was made by my grandfather." He sihed and then picked up the arrow and ran his fingers along the carvings. "You see these mountains? The rivers? The clouds? What does this look like to you?"

"It looks like Kwangsi," the inspector said.

Mr. Zhao nodded. "This is our home," he said. "Our people are made of the mountains, carved out hard and strong. You can't imagine what it was like when we were forced to leave."

"Is that why you killed you daughter with this arrow?" the inspector asked. "Because she had dishonored the family in some way?"

"No," the old man said earnestly. "She was our pearl. A good girl who worked hard. I know I was mad when I found out about the boy, but she was old enough to marry. Past age to marry! If she had requested the match, I would have given my blessing. My wife says the boy was good quality."

"But someone killed her," Inspector Gong said. "And using this arrow was not random. You said it was a family heirloom. If you didn't kill her with it, who else had access to it?"

The old man went silent.

Inspector Gong turned to the man's wife. "Will you tell me? Will you get justice for your daughter?"

She held her hand to her lips, trying to control her crying, but her tears flowed freely.

"Is it a family member?" Inspector Gong asked. "A brother? An uncle? Who was your daughter afraid of?"

"Afraid?" Mrs. Zhao asked. "What makes you think she was afraid? She never said anything."

Inspector Gong pulled out the stack of letters and turned to the one with the passage Lady Li had translated.

"She was writing love letters to Wang Bolin in English so they wouldn't get in trouble," he explained. "In one of the letters she said, 'if he comes back, I don't know how I will survive.' Any idea who she was talking about?"

Mr. and Mrs. Zhao looked at each other and shook their heads.

"We don't know," Mr. Zhao said. "She never said she was afraid of anyone in the legation. She always said she was very happy there."

Inspector Gong nodded. He wasn't surprised. It was common for children to keep things from their parents so as not to cause them worry.

"Who was she sending money to?" Inspector Gong asked.

"She sent money to us, of course," Mr. Zhao said. "She was a good daughter."

"There was someone else," Inspector Gong explained. "In another letter, she specifically says that she was late to work because she was sending money to Jiaolong. Who is Jiaolong?"

Mr. Zhao froze and the color drained from Mrs. Zhao's face.

"Tell me," Inspector Gong ordered, banging his hand on the table.

"Jiaolong is dead to us," Mr. Zhao finally said through gritted teeth.

"*Who is he*?" Inspector Gong asked firmly.

"He is...*was* our son," Mr. Zhao admitted with hatred in his eyes. "I disowned that bastard years ago."

"Why?" Inspector Gong asked.

"He is an opium eater," he said. "He spends all his time and money in opium dens with whores and gangsters."

"Why didn't you tell me this before?" Inspector Gong asked. "Didn't you think it was important?"

"No!" the father spat. "We have not seen him in years! We had no idea that Weilin was sending him money! Why would she? She was just a girl when we sent him away. She saw what he did to us. How he nearly destroyed us. Why would she allow that scoundrel in her life?"

"You tell me," the inspector said. "Why would your daughter remain in contact with her brother?"

"He must have gone to her," the father said. "Maybe he threatened her. When he learned she had a good job, he must have pressured her to give him money."

Inspector Gong nodded. It was possible. "Did you give your son the arrow?" he asked.

"No," Mr. Zhao said. "I gave it and the matching bow to Weilin. It was supposed to pass from father to son, but after I threw him out of the house, I gave them to Weilin. She took them with her when she went to live at the legation."

"So how did your son get a hold of it?" Inspector Gong asked.

"You think our son used the arrow to kill our daughter?" the man asked. Mrs. Zhao burst into wailing.

"It makes sense," Inspector Gong said. "You insulted him by giving the arrow to Weilin, so he insulted you by killing her with it."

Mr. Zhao leaned back in his seat. His face turned green, then he ran to the door and vomited in the street. Then he wandered outside and ripped his clothes, screaming curses. His wife ran after him, screaming out her pain.

Inspector Gong followed them. His men started to

approach the couple, but he motioned for them to hold back. The old couple were not merely putting on a show, they were truly grieving. He needed to see what they would do. What they would say.

They cursed themselves. They cursed their son. They cursed the Gods for failing to protect such a filial daughter. Interestingly, though, they also cursed Mr. Gibson, Weilin's employer.

"Why Mr. Gibson?" Inspector Gong asked as he walked along beside them.

"It is all his fault," Mr. Zhao said. "It all began with him."

"In what way?" Inspector Gong pushed.

"Don't you know?" Mr. Zhao asked. "He is the biggest opium importer in China!"

"What?" Inspector Gong asked. "How do you know that?"

"Everyone with a child addicted to opium knows," he said.

"Then why did you let her work for him?" the inspector asked.

"I didn't know until she was already working there," he said. "I knew the missionaries were helping her get a job in the legation, but I didn't know it was with *him*. After I found out, the job was too good for her to quit, and I thought it was a way for him to pay off part of his debt to me. But now, that bastard has cost me both of my children!"

"Calm down," Inspector Gong said. "Let's focus on your son right now. Where can I find him?"

"Death to the opium runners!" Mr. Zhao shouted as he stood and raised his fist. "Death to the British! Death to the foreigners!"

"Death to the foreigners!" many voices echoed.

Inspector Gong looked around and realized the Zhaos

had moved down to a busy intersection and large crowd of people had gathered around them. He ran up to Mr. Zhao. "Stop this now or I will have you arrested!"

"You protect the foreigners while they kill our children with drugs!" Mr. Zhao screamed. "You are no better than them!"

The crowed began to jeer and raise their fists.

"Burn the legation!" Mr. Zhao yelled.

"Burn the legation!" the crowed echoed.

Inspector Gong motioned for his men to arrest Mr. Zhao, but as they moved in, the crowd surrounded him and his wife.

"You wish to punish me when my daughter is dead?" Mr. Zhao yelled. "You'll have to kill me before you can arrest me!"

The crowd cheered and moved in even more tightly around Mr. Zhao. The people began to move toward the legation and grow in size.

Inspector Gong stood back and let them pass. He couldn't take on the whole crowd himself.

"What do we do, boss?" one of his men asked.

"You, run ahead and warn the legation guards that the crowd is coming," he told him. "And, you," he addressed the other one. "Hurry to the Foreign Ministry and tell Prince Kung to send a full contingent of guards to the legation immediately. Hurry!"

Inspector Gong stayed with the crowd to make sure Mr. Zhao didn't escape.

He could do nothing as the crowd erupted into a riot.

13

*I*nspector Gong had no idea what he was going to do. He was alone and unarmed against an ever-growing angry mob. His only goal for now was to keep Mr. and Mrs. Zhao in his sight. Mr. Zhao would have to be arrested for inciting a riot. Something that would only make the people more angry, but Inspector Gong had to do his job.

As the crowd approached the legation, he saw the guards hurrying the few foreigners who were outside the gates inside. Then the guards locked the gates and held their rifles in a defensive position, ready to fire if necessary.

Of course all it took was one anxious finger, one boy itching for a fight, or one terrified soldier with sweaty palms to set off a massacre. Inspector Gong knew that the men who were holding the gate had been trained not to fire. To use deadly force only as a last resort. But as a former soldier himself, he also knew that training tended to be tossed to the wind when young men were afraid.

"This is Chinese land!" he heard Mr. Zhao shout to the

guard even though the guard wouldn't understand him. "You are in China! This is not your land! You get out of here!"

"Get out of China!" some of the people yelled. "Death to the White Devils!"

They raised their fists in anger and crowded the guards. It was like there was an invisible line between the guards and the rioters that no one dared cross, but they inched as close as possible, as though dancing with death.

The growing crowd pushed and shoved, moving the whole group closer to the line of no return. Inspector Gong slowly, carefully worked his way through the crowd. If he could just get to Mr. Zhao. If he could pull him back, he was sure the rest of the crowd would follow. Whatever happened, he had to protect Mr. Zhao. If the man was killed, he would become a martyr. A rallying point for a war that he would be unable to stop.

Inspector Gong inched his way closer. He reached his hand out and grasped Mr. Zhao's collar.

Mr. Zhao turned and looked at him, his eyes wide with surprise.

Inspector Gong shook his head. "Don't do this," he said.

"It's too late," Mr. Zhao said.

From the corner of his eye, Inspector Gong some something fly by. As he looked up, he saw it. A brick. It flew from the back of the crowd, over all their heads, and was heading straight for one of the guards. Inspector Gong watched as it seemed to move in slow motion. He looked ahead to see where it would land, and saw a young soldier, not more than twenty, with his rifle cocked, his eye on the sight, his brow sweaty, his hands shaking ever so slightly. He was aiming squarely at Mr. Zhao.

As the brick hit its target, he heard the rifle crack.

"No!" Inspector Gong shouted. He closed his eyes and pushed Mr. Zhao out of the way as the crowd erupted into screams.

Some of the crowd rushed the guards. More rifle shots rang out. Inspector Gong hit the ground. He felt someone step on his leg, then his arm. He opened his eyes and met those of Mr. Zhao.

Mr. Zhao was cowering, with his hands protecting his head.

Inspector Gong pushed him away. "Get out of here!" he yelled. Mr. Zhao nodded and tried to get to his feet, but then Inspector Gong grabbed him by the shirt and pulled him close. "But I will find you. I promise."

Mr. Zhao looked more terrified of Inspector Gong than the mob that threatened to crush them both. He pulled away, got to his feet, and then disappeared through the crowd.

Inspector Gong grunted as he forced himself to stand. He was injured, but he wasn't exactly sure where or how badly. He hurt everywhere and his head was ringing. But he forced himself to stand and fight. He grabbed a man by the shoulder and threw him to the ground. "Stay down!" he yelled. He shouldered past two more people. Someone pulled his queue, so he turned around and punched the person in the face.

Slowly and violently, he worked his way to the front of the crowd where the rioters were battling with the legation guards. He would hate himself for it later, but he had to take the side of the guards and repel his own people. As he got to the front, one of the guards tried to butt him in the face with his rifle, but Inspector Gong dodged it just in time. He then turned and pushed one of the rioters away. The guard stared at the inspector for a moment, confused as to why a Chinese would be defending him. Then realization washed over him as he recognized the inspector from his visits to the legation with Prince Kung. The inspector gave the guard a nod, and together they worked to push the crowd back away from the gate. They had to keep the mob from pressing in against it. It was strong, but it could not withstand the angry pressure from hundreds of determined people.

Inspector Gong did not know how long they had been fighting, but he could feel his body wearing out. He took a punch to the gut, and another to the face. But he stood his ground.

Finally, he heard the sound of a trumpet, signaling the arrival of the imperial guard. The rioters immediately dispersed. The guards grabbed as many people as they could and threw them into cages bound for the Ministry of Justice. Most of them would simply be interrogated, tortured, and then released, but no one wanted to go home with one less finger or ear.

Once Inspector Gong no longer had to fight, he let himself relax, just a bit, and leaned against the gate. The guard he had been fighting with patted him on the shoulder and then reached out to shake his hand. Inspector Gong tried to lift his hand to shake, but he felt a pain shoot through his body. He looked down, and saw that his arm was dripping with blood.

He stumbled back. He heard the guard shout something he didn't understand. And then he only saw black.

"*A*m I in danger?" he heard someone ask.

Inspector Gong slowly opened his eyes. He was in a warm dark room. He wasn't sure where he was, but it seemed familiar.

"I don't think so," he heard a voice reply.

He sat up and winced. He looked down and saw that his ribs were wrapped with gauze, as was his left arm. He stood up and his whole body tried to seize, but he forced himself to take a step. He grunted out loud, but he managed to get across the room to a dressing table with a mirror.

"Ai-yo!" he exclaimed when he saw his black eye and busted lip.

"But what will I do if they turn on us?" he heard Lady Li ask.

Lady Li! Was he in Lady Li's home? How did he end up here? He walked over to the door and opened it slightly. He saw her sitting there, worry etched on her face. But then he saw someone take her hand. It was the hand of a man. She did not pull away.

"I will always protect you," he heard Prince Kung say.

Prince Kung! Of course it was him. He knew that the prince and Lady Li had once been in love, many years ago. Is that why she had rejected him the other day. Had the prince begun courting her again? Had the empress finally given them her blessing to wed? Why had the prince not told him?

He pulled the door open the whole way and stepped out.

Lady Li looked up and then jerked her hand away from Prince Kung's hand. "Inspector Gong!" she cried. She jumped up and ran to his side. "Are you all right?" she asked. "I had my personal physician come and care for you, but he said he wouldn't know the extent of your injuries until you woke up. I'll send for him to come back."

"Stop fussing, woman," he said more harshly than he intended. "I'm fine." She looked hurt, but pressed her lips together in a thin line and said nothing. He tried to ignore the tug at his heart at seeing her pain.

The prince stood and walked over to him. "You are lucky she lived so close," the prince said. "And that we had a safe place to bring you. You took one hell of a beating. A bullet grazed your arm."

"It's nothing," the inspector said as he went back into the room to find his shirt. "I need to find Zhao. And his son."

"His son?" Lady Li asked. "The Zhaos have a son?"

"Yes," he said. He tried not to wince as he raised his arm to pull his shirt and robe around himself. "The Jiaolong person," he explained. "It's their son. Mr. Zhao disowned him many years ago for being an opium addict and gangster."

"So you think the son might have killed his sister?" Lady Li asked.

Inspector Gong nodded. "That's why Zhao started the riot," he said. "Well, sort of. He blames himself for his son killing his daughter. But he blames Mr. Gibson most of all."

"What does Mr. Gibson have to do with it?" she asked.

"Mr. Gibson is apparently the biggest opium importer in the legation," he said. He looked at Prince Kung accusingly. "Did you know about this?"

The prince nodded slowly. "I did. You know that opium imports are legal under the Treaty of Tientsin"

"Legal or not," the inspector said, "Zhao blames him for getting his son addicted and getting his daughter killed. I'm sure there are many parents out there who will sympathize with him."

"I'm sure we arrested quite a few sympathizers today," the prince said. "But Zhao was not among them."

"I saw him escape," Inspector Gong said. "He's old. I didn't want to see him injured in the skirmish."

"I have my men looking for him now," the prince said. "I am sure he will turn up soon."

"I'll try to find the son, then," the inspector said. "He is my chief suspect right now."

"You better make an arrest soon," the prince said. "I don't care if he is guilty or not. If you can't find the son, then charge Wang."

"What?" Lady Li asked. "You can't be serious."

"I am," the prince said. "The British have threatened to send warships to blow open the port if Hart doesn't reopen soon. He won't without my approval, but he could face a court martial. We need to solve this crime now."

Lady Li shuddered and collapsed in a nearby chair. "They are threatening to bombard the Dagu Fort?" she asked. The prince nodded, and she hid her face in her sleeve. "It's happening again!" she cried.

Inspector Gong remembered that Lady Li had been serving at the Forbidden City the last time the foreigners bombed the Dagu Fort and stormed the Forbidden City.

She had been forced to flee for her life along with the imperial family.

"Do not fear, Lady Li," the prince said. "As long as you and Inspector Gong name a killer, we can arrest him and then reopen the ports."

"But we cannot name an innocent person!" she said. "We need more time."

"You may be out of time, Lady Li," the prince said. He then turned to leave. "I must return to the Foreign Ministry. The situation is changing by the minute."

"But who will protect us if the British attack?" she asked, standing and chasing after him.

"I will place two of my own guards outside your door," the prince said. "I will not abandon you."

Lady Li looked at the prince fondly as he left. Inspector Gong crossed his arms and let out a breath. She looked at him as if she had forgotten he was there.

"Are you sure you are all right?" she asked walking back to his side. "I can send for the doctor again. It's no trouble."

"I'm fine," he said as he too headed toward the door.

"Where are you going?" she asked.

"I have to find Jiaolong," he said.

"So you are still going to try to find the real killer?" she asked.

"For now," he said. "Until the prince says our time is up I will continue to do my job."

"What can I do to help?" she asked.

"You have done enough," he said as he opened the door.

"What do you mean by that?" she asked.

He sighed, trying to push his jealousy aside and think rationally. His arm twinged in pain. "Nothing. You have done what you can. Now I need to do my job."

"Are you coming back?" she asked.

"Why?" he asked in return, looking at her. "Why do you need me? You have the prince to protect you."

Her expression hardened. "I will not be made to feel guilty for protecting my family," she said through gritted teeth.

"Then I supposed there is nothing left to say," he said as he stepped through the door.

"Damn you, Inspector Gong!" she screamed at him.

"You're not the first woman to say that to me," he yelled back. "And you won't be the last!"

She slammed the gate shut behind him and locked it.

14

$\mathcal{A}$s Inspector Gong headed out to find his men, he couldn't believe he had done it again. He had stormed out on Lady Li. By the Gods, when he found Jiaolong he was going to beat the shit out him just because he could.

He met up with his men at an inn near his house. Together they plotted out where all the opium dens where in the area that they knew of. Of course, opium dens opened and closed frequently. And Jiaolong might not even be in an opium den in the area. Peking was huge. They could never check all of them. And after checking only one or two, word would start to spread that Inspector Gong was looking for him and he could flee. He wished he had a better plan for tracking the boy down, but he was out of ideas and out of time.

As he looked at the map, he noticed there was an opium den very near to Lady Li's mansion. He had no reason to think that Jiaolong would be there, but it was as good a place to start as any.

When they arrived, it was clear even from the outside that this opium den was nicer than most. In this neighborhood near many Manchu mansions, their clients were probably wealthy. The building was in good repair, and the street outside the building was clean. On one side of the door stood a large man, a guard. On the other side of the door was a beautiful young woman holding a pipe. She was the bait, the advertisement for the opium den to entice customers.

As Inspector Gong approached the building, the man flexed his muscles, but the woman gave him an enticing smile.

"Care for a smoke, my lord?" she asked.

"I'm no lord," he said. "I'm looking for someone."

"I can be someone," she said with a wink.

"I'm sure you could be," he said. "But this is part of an investigation."

She took on a more serious tone. "We don't want trouble," she said.

"Nor do I," he said. "I'm looking for Zhao Jiaolong. Do you know him?"

She shook her head. "I don't know that name," she said. "But you know most people here give fake names. Do you know what he looks like?"

He shook his head. "I only know his father. I need to go in and have a look. I might see someone familiar."

"As long as you promise to behave," she said sweetly, opening the door.

The opium den was quite nice inside, like he suspected. The kangs were large and separated by privacy curtains. The rooms were dark, so the patrons could sleep. There were also people gaming and women serving drinks and food. Some of the women were also prostitutes and a few of the men were there conducting business. The people were all well-dressed and clean, not the type one usually found in opium dens. There were even high-class women patrons partaking of the opium as well. Most of them were there in the company of a manservant for protection.

He had a feeling he was not going to find Jiaolong here. If he was living on the charity of his sister, the money wouldn't go far. He could get a lot more opium in a much shoddier place. He sighed, frustrated with himself. As he turned to leave, though, he bumped right into a woman he thought he had seen before.

She looked up at him, and her eyes went wide and her face went white. She turned and tried to flee, but he grabbed her arm.

"Do I know you?" he asked.

She just shook her head and tried to wrest free from his grasp. Then he suddenly remembered who she was.

"Concubine Swan?"

"No!" she cried. "Let me go! I have done nothing."

"I know it is you," he said. Even though he had only seen her a couple of times before, and never for very long, he knew it was her. "What are you doing here? Lady Li is going to kill you."

"Shhhh!" she hissed. "Do you want to bring shame on her house? I am not this girl you say."

"Well, whatever name you go by here," he said, not letting go of her arm, "you are coming with me."

"No, please," she begged. "You are right. She will kill me!"

"What am I supposed to do?" he asked. "I can't leave you here. When you return, she will know you left the house. What excuse did you give her?"

"I...I didn't" she said, her head hanging in shame. "I just...left."

"She is going to lose her mind when he finds you are missing!" the inspector barked, shaking her by the arm.

"I know!" she cried. "But you don't...you don't understand! I need..."

"You need to eat opium?" he asked harshly. "Is your life in a mansion with no worries so terrible?"

"What do you know about it?" she demanded angrily. "My husband is dead. My baby is dead. My life is dead! Dead!" She began to cry as she beat against his chest with her tiny fists.

"Fine. Calm down," he said, putting his arms around her and comforting her. "I still don't know what I can do for you. You have to go home."

"Maybe I can help you," she said, looking up at him hopefully.

"What do you mean?" he asked.

"My mistress is letting me help with the investigation," she said. "I went with her to the legation. I speak English."

"So," he said. "How does that help either of us?"

"Why are you here?" she asked. "You weren't looking for me. Who were you looking for?"

"I was looking for Zhao Jiaolong, the brother of the woman who was murdered," he said.

Her eyes lit up. "I know where he is!" she said. "Protect me from my mistress, and I will tell you where he is."

"How do you know where he is?" he asked.

She tossed her head to the side and laughed. "People talk when they are in the cloud."

Inspector Gong grimaced. He shouldn't be involving her. But he needed to find the boy quickly.

"Fine," he said. "I have no idea how, but I will at least speak on your behalf to your lady."

Concubine Swan clapped her hands together and laughed. He wondered how old she was. In many ways, she still seemed very girlish.

"You can tell her you needed my help," she said. "That is why I had to leave the house."

"Sure," he said. "I needed your help to find an opium-addicted gangster. That's not going to get you in trouble at all."

"Shush!" she said slapping his arm. "She doesn't need to know the details."

"Fine," he said. "Let's get you home."

"Not now!" she said crossing her arms. "Someone could see me! And if the neighbors see you bringing me back, they will think the worst. Besides, I don't know the city well enough to tell you the name of the place. I will have to show you."

Inspector Gong rubbed the bridge of his nose. "You women are going to be the death of me."

"Come on," she said, pulling his arm. She went to the front door and talked to the proprietor. He nodded and then stepped outside. She pulled down a scarf from a rack by the door and wrapped it around her head.

"What are you doing?" he asked.

"I can't let anyone see me," she said. "The laoban went to find a sedan chair for us. I'll direct him where to go. Then you can return me home after dark."

"This is a terrible idea, you know," Inspector Gong said, but he had to admire her tenacity.

"I can't remember when I last felt so alive," she said.

The laoban opened the door and waved them out. Concubine Swan quickly exited and jumped into a waiting sedan chair. The chair bearer talked to her and she did her best to explain where she wanted to go. The chair bearer nodded. Inspector Gong hopped into the chair next to her and told his men to follow them.

The chair was cramped, so he couldn't help but be uncomfortably close to Concubine Swan. She didn't seem to mind and practically tried to snuggle next to him. As the bearer picked up the front of the chair, they were both unceremoniously tossed back in the seat. Inspector Gong couldn't help but let out a groan of pain as he held his ribs.

"Oh! You must be in so much pain!" Concubine Swan fussed, doing her best to move away from him.

"I've had worse," he said. "I've been in the military."

"So I've heard," she said. "I heard the riot was very violent. You were lucky."

"I'll be fine," he said. "It's all part of the job."

She bit her lower lip and leaned in close. "You are so brave," she said.

He leaned back. "Concubine Swan," he said. "I brought you with me to help on the case. Nothing more."

"Is that how you seduced Lady Li?" she asked, pouting her lips. "I know there is more going on with you two. But she can't have you. She's a lady. I'm a nobody. I could be whatever you want me to be." She leaned in and closed her eyes.

"Concubine Swan..." he started to say, but the chair jerked forward and he nearly fell out of the seat. "Ai-yo!" he nearly screamed as he grabbed his ribs.

He stumbled out of the chair into the street. One of his men grabbed him by the arm he had been shot in and pulled him to his feet. He gritted his teeth to keep from crying like a baby, the pain was so intense.

"Damnit, man!" he yelled. "What the hell is wrong with you?"

"Sorry, boss," the man said, doing his best to hide a snicker. He looked around and noticed the rest of his men were chuckling as well. He looked back and saw Concubine Swan leaning out of the chair.

He closed the flap of the chair in front of her. "Stay here," he ordered her. Then he turned to his men. "Follow me."

The house where this opium den was located was more what he expected. It was a decrepit old dwelling from the outside and there were no guards or fine ladies to welcome them.

When he opened the door and entered, he was hit by a wave of smoke and the smell of unwashed humans. There was only one large room, but large was a generous word. There were wooden slats along three walls, and people, mostly men in various stages of undress, lounged on top of them. As his eyes adjusted, he realized that under the slats along the floor laying on bamboo mats were more half naked people.

An elderly man shuffled up to the inspector. "Please," he said in a soft voice. "We are simple folk. We don't want trouble."

"And you won't have any," the inspector said. "As long as you hand over Zhao Jiaolong right now."

"Oh, I don't know my patrons' names," the man said. "Privacy is important for my business, you understand."

"I understand that if you don't hand over Zhao Jiaolong right now," the inspector said, raising his voice for all the patrons to hear, "I am going arrest every person in this disgusting rat nest."

Several of the patrons tried to rouse themselves from their drug-induced stupor, but were slow going of it.

"Here," one raspy voice called out. "He's here." The man raised his hand and pointed to the man next to him."

"You bastard," the other man said as he slid of the wooden slat and shuffled toward the door.

Inspector Gong tried to grab him, but the man pushed him away. Normally, it would have been a feeble attempt, but with his injuries, he was easily pushed away. Two of his men went to grab Jiaolong, but he slipped between them and shot out the door.

"Grab him!" Inspector Gong yelled. He headed toward the door, expecting Jiaolong to be long gone, but instead he saw him lying face down on the ground with Concubine Swan standing over him.

"I stopped him!" she yelled.

"How?" Inspector Gong asked as he signaled for his men to collect the boy off the ground. "You were supposed to stay in the cart!"

"You were taking so long, I was worried you weren't going to be able to find him. So I was about to come in to help you when he ran out. I figured if he was running, he might be escaping, so I just stuck out my foot and tripped him."

Concubine Swan beamed. Inspector Gong agreed internally that she did a good job, but he knew better than to encourage her.

"Get back in the cart," he said firmly.

"But didn't I do a good job?" she asked, begging for his approval. "I helped you..."

"Get in the cart!" he yelled.

He could see her heart break right in front of him as the

smile melted from her face. She turned and got back into the cart, but he could already hear her crying.

He turned to his men. "Take him to the Ministry of Justice. I must see the lady home first."

They nodded and dragged the boy away.

He turned back to the cart to get in, but when he did, he saw the curtain on the other side of the chair flapping in the wind.

Concubine Swan was gone.

15

*B*y the next day, Eunuch Bai still had not returned. Lady Li paced in her chambers, unsure of what to do. That the foreigners had threatened war had her nerves on edge. She almost didn't want to wait to see what happened; she wanted to get out of Peking. But how? As a woman, she couldn't travel China alone, and she had no man to escort her. Also, Popo was still very weak. Even though her health had improved since she moved in with Lady Li, she was feeble. She wasn't sure the old woman could survive an arduous journey.

There was Prince Kung. He had said he would not abandon her if things went wrong, but just how much could she rely on that? She trusted the prince with her life and counted him a friend, but he had his own family to attend to. And if he suddenly needed to flee, would he have time to send for Lady Li? She didn't think she should solely rely on him for assistance. She needed another plan, but she had nowhere to turn.

Even that insufferable Inspector Gong was not an option. She didn't know much about his family situation, but she doubted his family would want him to spend any effort trying to help a Manchu, especially if the tide of popular opinion turned on them. He wouldn't want to make his family a target by allying himself with a Manchu woman.

She wondered if the women who called her a friend in the foreign legation would be willing to help her. Probably not. They had been kind to her, but if war broke out between China and the foreign countries, they wouldn't want to appear to be cavorting with the enemy.

Truly, Lady Li had never felt so alone.

She thought about how helpful—if blunt—Concubine Swan had been when they were visiting the foreign ladies. She had known that Concubine Swan was well educated, but she had never considered whether the girl had any practical skills or common sense. In her position, Concubine Swan would have little use for either one. She simply did what she was told. Lady Li wondered if Concubine Swan might have any ideas about what they could do. She walked down the hall and knocked on Concubine Swan's door.

There was no answer.

She knocked again. Again she was met with only silence. Surely the girl was not lost in an opium daze this early in the morning.

"Concubine Swan!" Lady Li demanded. "Open this door."

Finally, the door opened a crack, and Concubine Swan's maid peeked through.

"Can I help you, madam?" the maid asked quietly.

"I wish to speak with Concubine Swan," Lady Li said.

"I'm afraid she is not feeling well," the maid said. "Perhaps later..."

"Open this door, now," Lady Li said firmly, pushing the door open and entering the room. The room was completely dark.

"What is wrong with you?" Lady Li asked the maid. "Light the braziers and open the windows."

The maid simply trembled before her.

"What is going on?" Lady Li asked. "What is wrong with Concubine Swan?"

The maid crumpled to the floor, knocking her forehead to the floor. "I'm sorry, my lady. I'm sorry."

Lady Li threw the door open to let more light into the room. As her eyes adjusted, she looked around for Concubine Swan. She was not there! She ran over to the bed and threw open the curtains. The bed had not been slept in.

"Where is she?" Lady Li shrieked. "Where is Concubine Swan?"

"I don't know," the maid wept. "She threatened to beat me, to have me fired, to claim I was a thief if I didn't open the back gate for her yesterday. She said she would only be away for a few hours. She never returned, and I was terrified."

Lady Li grabbed the girl by the ear. "You stupid girl!" she screamed. "She has been gone for more than a day? Out on the streets? Alone!"

"I'm sorry, my lady," the maid cried.

"Where did she go?" Lady Li asked, still pinching the girl's ear.

"I...I..."

"Where?"

"An opium den, my lady," the maid finally admitted.

In her shock, Lady Li let go of the girl and covered her mouth. "An opium den?" she asked. "Where would she even know how to find such a place?"

The maid continued to cry and kowtow at Lady Li's feet. "I believe she saw it when you took her to the legation," she said. "From the window of the sedan chair. She said it was very near. Only a few houses down."

"Why didn't you tell me?" Lady Li asked. She glanced up and saw that other servants were peeking in the door, trying to find out what had happened. They quickly scattered when they saw her looking at them. This was a disaster. The servants were terrible gossips. The news that Concubine Swan had snuck out to an opium den would be all over the neighborhood within hours.

"She threatened me," the girl explained. "If I was cast out as a thief, I would never find another job. And she said she would be back soon. I thought she would come back before you knew she was gone."

"But that was yesterday," Lady Li said. "Why didn't you tell me when she didn't return. She could be dead!"

"I know, my lady," the maid said. "I became even more afraid. How was I to tell you?"

Lady Li grunted and stormed out of the room. The maid would have to be fired. Someone that stupid and untrustworthy could not remain in her household. But what was she to do about Concubine Swan now? The maid said the opium house was very close. But she could not go there on her own. And she had no male servant to send whom she could trust.

Damn that Eunuch Bai—how dare he abandon her!

She would have to send for Inspector Gong. She was none too pleased with him right now. And she didn't know if he would return even if she did ask. She had cursed him when he last left the house. But this was not a personal request, but a professional one. If she had to, she would hire him to find the girl.

She went to her office and wrote a note to Inspector Gong requesting his assistance. As she wrote, tears formed in the corner of her eyes. What if the girl was dead? She couldn't bear it if something terrible had happened to her. She knew that Concubine Swan was miserable. She knew that the girl had become addicted to opium, but she had looked the other way. She had failed the girl as her mistress, as her protector. In trying to keep her safe, she had only kept her in a cage. It was only a matter of time before she tried to escape.

She had not yet finished the letter when a different maid knocked on her door.

"My lady," the maid said.

"What is it?" Lady Li asked, wiping her tears.

"Inspector Gong is here," she said. "And he has Concubine Swan with him."

Lady Li could not speak out of shock. She flew from her office to the main courtyard. She could hardly believe her eyes when she saw Inspector Gong there with Concubine Swan.

Concubine Swan was smiling, and Lady Li felt herself fly into a rage. She stomped toward Concubine Swan and slapped her face. Concubine Swan held her hand to her cheek and began to cry.

"You dare come back here!" Lady Li yelled. "You sneak out, go to an opium den. You are gone all night! I thought you were dead! You'll wish you were!"

Lady Li raised her hand to strike the concubine again, but she felt Inspector Gong grab her arm.

"Be calm," he said softly. "She is alive, and unharmed."

Lady Li took a step back and wiped her face with her sleeve. "Go from my sight," she said, a little out of breath.

Concubine Swan's maid ran to her and helped her to her room.

Inspector Gong placed a hand on Lady Li's shoulder. He didn't say anything, but just his touch helped calm her.

"Do you have any idea what this means?" Lady Li asked. "What will happen when word gets out about what she has done?"

"I know this will reflect badly on your family," he said.

"Badly?" she asked, looking at him. "It could ruin us. All this time I have worried about my actions reflecting badly on my children. I never thought that Concubine Swan would be the one to put everything in jeopardy."

"Surely the actions of a concubine will not ruin the lives of your daughters?" Inspector Gong asked. "She is not their mother. Everyone knows that keeping the concubine after your husband's death was a kindness on your part."

She shakes her head. "I cannot know how this will play out," she said. "But we will not be spared some sort of fall-out. Someone will pay for this, one way or another."

"Will it help if you find out what she learned, what she did?" he asked. "She helped with the investigation greatly."

"I wish I had the energy to care about that right now," she said, finally looking up at him. "Eunuch Bai is gone. He has abandoned me."

"I cannot believe that," Inspector Gong said, his eyes wide. "That man is eternally devoted to you."

"That is what I thought too," she said, shaking her head. "But he has been gone for days and has sent no word."

"But why would he leave you?" he asked.

She looked at him for a moment and then scoffed. "You know why," she said finally.

"No," he said. "I cannot believe it. He knows you and I..."

He could not finish the sentence. They looked at each other for a moment, each trying to read the other person's mind.

"He knows," she finally said, not putting words to their feelings. "But here, in my own house? It was dangerous and stupid. He probably felt I was putting the whole household in danger and did not want to wait around to see it happen."

"I will set some of my men to look for him," he said. "Maybe...maybe something happened to him."

Lady Li sighed and closed her eyes. She rubbed her forehead. "I hadn't even considered that. In my selfishness, I thought only of myself. But you are right. What if he has been injured or kidnapped and I did nothing to help him?"

She could not stop the tears this time. Inspector Gong pulled her into his arms and she did not pull away. She did not care if the servants or her children saw. She needed this. She needed someone to comfort her. And she had the feeling he needed her too. Not in the carnal way he usually did, but in the familiar, safe way a man sometimes needs even if he does not put it to words. As he held her, with her head on his chest, she listened as his heartbeat slowed.

Finally, they forced themselves to part.

"Would you come to my office?" Lady Li asked. "You said she helped with the investigation."

"Only for a moment," he said with a nod. "I must get back as soon as possible."

She nodded to a maid as they entered the office. "Tea," she said. As they entered, she once again left the door open.

"Please, sit," she offered. "What have you found out?"

"The girl works fast," he said. "She claims she had not been to the opium house before. But she already had made some...friends."

Lady Li gulped and pursed her lips. "Was she whoring?" she asked through gritted teeth.

"I do not think so," he said as a maid poured them tea and then left the room. "But you will need to ask her the... delicate details."

"Go on, then," Lady Li said.

"Somehow, she knew where Zhao Jiaolong was. He was another opium house, barely a hole in the wall quite a distance away. I guess he has a loose tongue, and even she had heard of him at the house she was in."

"So you found him?" she asked. "What did he say? Did he kill his sister?"

"I have not had time to question him," Inspector Gong said. "After I captured him, Concubine Swan slipped away. I think she was afraid of what would happen when I returned her home."

"As she should have been," Lady Li said sharply.

"I was going to cover for her," he said. "Claim that I had asked her for help. But I guess you found out where she was somehow. When you started screaming about her being in an opium den, there was no point in denying it."

"I cannot believe you would lie to me for her," Lady Li said, leaning back and crossing her arms.

Inspector Gong smirked. "I do not know if I could have gone through with it. You needed to know."

"So she slipped away from you?" Lady Li said. "Then what?"

"I spent all night looking for her," he said. "I was frantic. I knew you would never forgive me if something happened to her. But this morning, I received a note from my brother. She had turned up at my home."

Lady Li couldn't help but laugh. "What must your mother have thought."

"I'm terrified to find out," he said, his mouth curved up

in a half-smile. "But you won't believe what Concubine Swan did."

"Tell me," she said, leaning forward.

"She pretended to be a legation servant, and they believed her! They let her inside even though it is supposed to be on lock down."

"No!" Lady Li gasped. "I can't believe it!"

"She did," he said. "Before she went to my home, she went to the Gibsons' house and spoke with their servants. She claims that they told her that they all knew that Mr. Gibson was taking the girl to his bed, even though she was unwilling."

"So...he was raping her?" Lady Li asked, horrified.

"He probably doesn't see it that way," Inspector Gong said. "She probably submitted out of fear of losing her job."

"That poor girl," Lady Li said. "So he might have been the man she was afraid of, the one she wrote about in her letter. And he could be the father of her child."

"It is possible," he said with a nod. "We have no way of knowing, but here is the most interesting part. The maid said that she was certain Mr. Gibson was home when the girl was killed."

"But his wife said they were at a play that night, all of them," Lady Li said.

"Maybe she is covering for him," he said. "Or could he have slipped away without her knowledge?"

"I don't know," Lady Li said. "I have never been to a western play. At Chinese opera performances, though, the men and women are separated. Perhaps western audiences are separated as well."

"Maybe you can find out," he said.

Lady Li sighed. "I don't know. I can't get into the legation right now. They aren't allowing visitors."

"But the foreigners are allowed to leave, if they dare," he said. "If you invite the ladies here, you could talk to them more."

Lady Li nodded. "I can try, but I do not know that they will accept. I'm sure they are too afraid to leave their houses."

"Just do the best you can." Inspector Gong put down his cup and rose to leave. "I must go and interrogate Jiaolong. Do let me know if you learn anything more."

Lady Li nodded. Then she hesitated before speaking more. "Inspector Gong," she finally said as he was about to leave the room. "I...I must ask you...I'm sorry, I know this seems terribly odd. You are not married. Would you consider taking Concubine Swan?"

Her heart hurt to say the words, but she needed to ask before her courage failed her.

"She is Manchu," he said.

Lady Li waved him off. "A nobody. A widowed, childless concubine. I do not think anyone would stop you, in a legal sense."

He cleared his throat. "She is a lovely girl, and very clever," he said. "But I fear my family would never allow it. Not as a wife anyway. Not with her...history."

Lady Li nodded. "That is my eternal stumbling block to finding her a new husband," she said. "She is so young, but has already been through so much."

He nodded. "They would not let me take her as a wife, but if I was to marry a Han girl, they might not object to me taking her as a concubine."

Lady Li felt her heart hitch in her chest. "So you have been considering taking a wife?"

"My family is becoming quite insistent upon it," he said

with a shrug. "I do not think I can delay much longer. I...I did not know how to tell you."

She stammered for a moment and tried to smile as if the news was nothing to her. "It matters not to me," she lied. "It is not as if *I* could ever marry you."

"No," he said somewhat sadly. "No, I don't suppose you could."

As their eyes locked, Lady Li's heart frozen in her chest. So she was not the only person who had entertained thoughts of them being together and found it impossible. Neither of them could ever hope to overcome the social rules keeping them apart.

"Good luck to you," she finally said softly. "Whoever she is, I hope she makes you happy."

He reached up and gently stroked Lady Li's cheek. "You know she won't."

$\mathcal{I}$nspector Gong was irritated he had spent the night searching for Concubine Swan instead of interrogating Jiaolong, but the boy had been so lost in opium he probably wouldn't have been able to answer any questions anyway. At least Concubine Swan was safe, and had found out some interesting information. He wasn't sure how the knowledge that Mr. Gibson had impregnated the girl would be useful, but any information that could help them solve this case faster was appreciated.

But what would Lady Li do with Concubine Swan now? He couldn't believe she had offered to sell her to him. He should have told her he would think about it, talk to his mother about it. After all, Concubine Swan was beautiful, smart, and flat-footed. True, she was Manchu and previously married, but if his mother was desperate enough for him to marry, she just might be persuaded to accept the girl.

But taking Lady Li's own servant as his wife? Would he ever be able to perform his husbandly duty with her and not think of Lady Li? Did Concubine Swan know about the...extent of his relationship with Lady Li? Could she be a good and dutiful wife to him if she did? Could he be a good husband to her with the shadow of Lady Li lurking behind them?

As Inspector Gong approached the Ministry of Justice, he shook his head to rid himself of such troublesome thoughts. This was why he had never allowed a woman into his life before. Nothing but distractions.

He stomped down the dark stairwell to the dank hallway below. The fetid smell infected his nose and the scurrying of rats sent chills down his spine. Even though his work had brought him here countless times, he was always glad to leave it. He couldn't imagine having to spend the night here.

As he opened the door to Jiaolong's cell, he was surprised to find the boy sleeping on the pile of damp, moldy hay in the corner. He looked worse than the day before, sweaty yet shivering. Inspector Gong walked over and gave him a good kick before dragging him to his feet.

"Get the hell up," he said as he pushed him up against a wall.

The boy's eyes opened, but they still had a foggy, listless gaze to them, as if he were incapable of lifting his lids all the way. Just how much opium had he had, the inspector wondered. He had been locked up for over twelve hours. He should not still be in the cloud.

The boy rubbed his eyes and his head lolled a bit. Inspector Gong gave him a slap.

"Wake up," he demanded. "Do you know why you are here? Where you even are?"

The boy sighed. "What does it matter?" he asked. "Here? There? All life is a cage."

"Who put you in that cage?" the inspector asked as he paced back and forth like a tiger, trying to intimidate the boy. Well, he could now see that Jiaolong wasn't exactly a boy. He had to be nearly thirty.

"If the universe sees fit to cage me, there is no point in trying to escape," Jiaolong lamented.

"Do you know why you are here?" Inspector Gong asked again.

"I don't know. My father sent you for me?" he guessed halfheartedly.

Inspector Gong smirked. "Why would he do that? Your father disowned you, didn't he?"

"Ahh," the boy said, his eyes lighting up for the first time. "So you do know the bastard? What did you think of him?"

"It doesn't matter what I think," the inspector said. "What do you think of your family?"

Jiaolong waved him away. "It doesn't matter. I am his son. He will have to have me back eventually."

"I'm not so sure about that," the inspector said. "He seemed to think your sister was good enough to give her the family heirlooms."

That finally got a reaction from the boy. He crossed his arms and his nostrils flared. "She is just a girl, a worthless girl. She cannot replace me."

"But she was supporting you," Inspector Gong said. "She was paying for your little opium habit, wasn't she? She was also supporting your parents while you laid on your back all day. I think you were the useless one."

Jiaolong attempted to jump up and get in Inspector Gong's face, but he was uneasy moving so quickly and the inspector easily pushed him back down.

"Piss off, little man," Inspector Gong said. "You can hardly stand, much less fight me. Just tell me what I want to know. Tell me about your sister."

"What is to tell?" Jiaolong asked, nearly falling back into the chair. "She's a worthless whore. So what if she gives me a bit of scraps of coin? She sold her body and her soul to that fat White Devil to get it."

Inspector Gong kept his face impassive. "What do you mean?" he asked. "She was just a maid."

"Just a maid?" the boy scoffed. "And girls in flower houses just serve tea."

"What makes you think she was whoring?" Inspector Gong asked.

"I can see it!" he said. "The last time she brought me money, she was very fat. She walked different. And that man, I saw him with her. I saw him touch her."

Inspector Gong was skeptical that Jiaolong would notice such subtle differences in his sister and know what they meant, but he supposed it was possible. If her parents and employer saw her regularly, they might not have noticed the subtle changes. But someone who only saw her every few months might think the changes were more dramatic. But he was more interested in when he might have seen Mr. Gibson acting inappropriate with the girl.

"When did you see Mr. Gibson with your sister?" he asked.

"That fat devil is the Opium King," he said. "This is all his fault. He is the reason I am like this!" He gripped his tattered and stained clothes pitifully. "If anyone should be dead, it is that man!"

"How did you know your sister was dead?" Inspector Gong asked.

"I hear it," he said, his head dropping. "I hear many things in the opium house. Everyone who is in the cloud, they tell everything."

"How did she die?" Inspector Gong asked.

"Do you know what she did?" he asked, looking up at the inspector with glassy eyes. "That whore? Do you know?"

"Tell me," the inspector said.

"She sold the bow and arrow. Gave them to a little pawn man for a few bits of cash. She told me so when she gave me money the last time."

The inspector had not known this. "And what did you think when she told you this?" he asked.

"She wanted to hurt me," Jiaolong said, tearing up. "Wanted me to know what she had done in order to 'help' me, she said. That bitch. Do I not suffer enough?"

Inspector Gong thought the boy did not suffer nearly enough, but did not say so.

"I threw the money back at her!" the boy continued. "I would not take it or any more from her. I would rather starve."

The boy was so skinny the inspector thought the boy was rather on his way. "And then what?" the inspector asked. "Did you go get the bow and arrow. Shoot her with it to send a message?"

Jiaolong sighed. "I wonder," he said wistfully. "I dream of it, when I am in the cloud. Weilin, she dishonored me. She dishonored the family. She dishonored herself. In the cloud, I take the arrow in my hand and plunge it into her chest. There is blood on my hands, but the family honor is preserved."

"Did you do it?" the inspector asked. "Are you admitting to killing your sister?"

"If I did it," he sighed, "then my father would never take me back. She was an unfaithful, unfilial daughter. But to my parents she was like a pearl in their hands. They would never forgive me if I punished her, even if it was for their benefit."

Inspector Gong was at the end of his patience. He growled as he grabbed Jialong by the shirt, pulled him from the floor, and slammed him into the wall. "Did you kill your sister?" he yelled. "Admit to me that you did it!"

"No!" Jiaolong cried, turning to jelly in Inspector Gong's grip. "It was only a dream!"

Inspector Gong let the boy go, and he crumpled to the floor, sobbing.

"Who did, then?" the inspector asked. The boy didn't respond except with tears, so Inspector Gong kicked him and then asked again. "Who killed your sister?"

"I don't know!" the boy cried as he curled up into a ball, clutching his belly.

"Damnit!" the inspector yelled as he stormed from the cell. He was so close. Why didn't the boy just admit to it? This could all be over. He should just charge the boy anyway. He was a worthless piece of shit. The boy's parents already thought he had done it. No one would miss him and this whole mess would come to an end.

He paced the hallway as he tried to decide what to do. He walked back to Jiaolong's cell, ready to charge him with the crime, but then he turned away. He didn't want to charge an innocent man with murder unless he had no other choice. The penalty would be beheading. He didn't want that on his conscience, no matter how worthless the boy was.

He then remembered that the girl's boyfriend was still locked up as well. He went to Bolin's cell and open the door. The young man was sitting there on the floor, his legs crossed as though he were meditating.

"Inspector!" Bolin cried out as he shuffled to his feet. "Where have you been? I thought you had forgotten me. Have you found the killer?"

"Who was Weilin afraid of?" the inspector asked without an explanation, he was so harried.

"What?" Bolin asked, confusion on his face. "She was afraid?"

"In one of her letters to you…" Inspector Gong reached into his many pockets searching for the letters. He nearly sighed with relief when he found them. He rifled through them, looking for the passage Lady Li had translated. "Here." He pointed to the words when he found them. "She says, 'if he comes back, I don't know how I will survive.' Who was she speaking of?"

He shook his head. "I…I'm not sure. Many people were causing her trouble. Mr. Gibson, her father, her worthless brother. Her uncle was coming to town as well."

"He uncle?" Inspector Gong asked. This was the first he was hearing about an uncle.

"Yes," Bolin explained. "He is a very hard man. Very traditional. He was furious over the loss of the family land. He blamed his brother, Weilin's father, for it. And he hated that Weilin worked for the foreigners. He thought it was a betrayal. He was also angry that Jialong had been disowned. He said that family should always come first."

"Could he have killed Weilin?" Inspector Gong asked. "To preserve the family honor?"

Bolin sighed. "I suppose it is possible. But I think any of them could have done it now."

"So do I," Inspector Gong said. "But I am running out of time. The foreigners are threatening war if we don't open the ports. But the prince doesn't want the ports opened until the killer is found. I need to name a killer. Now! Don't let it be you."

The boy gasped in horror. "Me? You know I did not do this. I love her!"

"You are lucky I found the brother," the inspector said. "Before I had him in custody the prince nearly ordered me to charge you with the crime."

Bolin leaned against the wall an all color drained from his face. "I didn't do it. I...love her. I will help you however I can."

"The uncle," Inspector Gong said. "I need to know who he is and where I can find him. I don't have all day to go searching."

The boy paced. "He is a Zhao, and he is younger than her father. I don't know his given name. But he is also a skilled woodcarver. Maybe he is in the artisan district."

Inspector Gong shook his head. "It's not enough. Do you know where she pawned the bow and arrow, the heirlooms from her father."

"Oh, yes," Bolin said, his eyes lighting up in remembrance. "She was very distraught over that. Her brother, the bastard, he needed more and more money. She couldn't earn enough. She had to support her parents and that worthless dog flea was eating more and more opium. It broke her heart to sell the bow and arrow, but she didn't know what else to do."

"Why didn't you tell me this before?" the inspector asked.

"I...I was afraid," he admitted. "If I told you all I knew, you would think I was guilty."

Inspector Gong exhaled slowly. The boy wasn't wrong. At least he was being honest now. "So where did she take them?" he asked.

"To a foreigner seller," he said. "Not Chinese. A Chinese shop would give her nothing. But these stupid foreigners, they pay top dollar for Chinese arts and crafts, family heirlooms, farm equipment! Can you believe it? Just junk, they sell it overseas. British people use it to decorate their houses."

Inspector Gong found this information surprising. Was there no end to the strange ways of foreigners? But he couldn't dwell on that now. "Who is the seller?"

"We call him Mr. Big," Bolin said. "He has a shop inside the legation. So not every Chinese can go there, but we who work in the legation, we sell things there. Some of the girls are very good at it. They go to the countryside and buy things from families very cheap. Embroidered shoes, wood door carvings, chopsticks, silly things. Then they sell them to Mr. Big and make a lot of money."

"Does he speak Chinese?" Inspector Gong asked.

"No, only English," he said. "That is why he only deals with legation Chinese."

"So whoever Mr. Big sold the bow and arrow to, that could be our killer," Inspector Gong said.

"I think so," Bolin said. "Did I help enough. Will you set me free?"

Inspector Gong opened the door to the cell. "Not yet," he said. "But you did well. I will be back."

He could hear Bolin whimper as he shut the door.

17

*L*ady Li was disgusted with herself. She was sick over it. The way she completely lost herself in her rage over Concubine Swan left her in a daze. How could she act that way? In front of her daughters? In front of Inspector Gong? In front of her servants?

Of course, she was within her right to be angry, and to even beat the girl. When her husband died, the ownership of Concubine Swan fell to her, and she was within her right to treat her however she wanted. No one would bat an eye if her husband had beat the concubine. But that was not Lady Li's way. She was not the sort of person who would give herself over to sudden surges of emotion. She was a calm, rational, logical person.

Or was she?

She wasn't sure anymore. She had given herself to Inspector Gong in a fit of passion as well. Something she had never imagined she would do. Since he came into her life, she hardly recognized herself. While it pained her heart to think of him marrying another woman, another part of her hoped he would. She needed him out of her life.

But she could no longer imagine her life without him in it.

She had been so lonely, so despondent before she met him. Even if he had brought her innumerable troubles, she was certainly no longer bored. But was he worth it? What would this...distraction cost her in the end? She was already tempting danger. Popo had said that the neighbor women were talking about how often Inspector Gong was coming to her home. How long would it be before their tongues started wagging about Concubine Swan? What would happen when the empress found out?

No, she could not risk everything for him. For a man, a Han, who could never mean anything more to her. She hoped he would marry, and soon. Then her life would go back to normal.

But what was she now to do about Concubine Swan?

Her opium addiction was getting out of control if she was willing to sneak out of the house to get it. She wasn't sure what to do about it, short of locking her in her room until the addiction ceased. But what of the reasons for her turning to opium in the first place? Lady Li sighed to herself. She had no idea how to help Concubine Swan lead a better, happier life. The thought of selling her to a man who would probably treat her poorly filled Lady Li with dread, but she feared she would soon have no choice.

Lady Li rubbed her stomach. All of her anxiety was making her nauseous. She was about to call for some ginger tea when there was a knock on her door.

"Enter," she said, expecting it to be her maid.

"My lady," came a familiar and dearly missed voice.

Lady Li spun around and could not stop tears from forming in her eyes. "Eunuch Bai!" she cried out.

There he stood, looking none the worse for wear, with a

small smile on his face. "I have returned with good news, my lady."

She quickly walked up to him. She wanted to embrace him, but it would not have been appropriate, so she wrung her hands instead. "Where have you been? Are you injured?"

"I am fine, my lady," he said. "I am sorry I did not tell you where I was going, but I feared you would try to stop me."

She reached out and took his hand. She pulled him to a chair. "Please, sit and tell me what happened."

He hesitated. "I couldn't..."

"I insist," she said, nearly pushing him into the chair as she sat next to him. She looked to the door and saw a surprised maid standing there. "Ginger tea," she said sharply. The maid quickly curtseyed and turned away. "Please, tell me everything," she said to Eunuch Bai.

"I heard about the riot," he said. "And I felt I had to do something. We have no one here we can rely on."

Lady Li nodded.

"But I did not think you would want me to make preparations for leaving," he said. "But should the worst happen, we cannot wait until the last minute."

"Popo suggested leaving China," Lady Li said. "But how? I wouldn't know where to start."

"That is what I went to find out," he said. "And I was successful. I found someone willing to buy your lands outside the city. With that money, and the money in your accounts, we could flee. I could wear Lord Yun's clothes, pose as your husband. We could change our names so no one would know you are a woman traveling without a male escort. It is quite easy to book passage on the Grand Canal to Hangchow. From Hangchow, we can book passage to Hong Kong."

"The British colony?" Lady Li asked. She hadn't even considered fleeing to Hong Kong, but it made sense. Hong Kong had been lost to the British in the Treaty of Nanking in 1842. It was still little more than a fishing village, but she had heard that the British were developing the island, making it more hospitable for British residents. She imagined it was becoming more like the foreign legation here in Peking.

"Exactly," Eunuch Bai said. "With your English, you could easily find us accommodation once we arrive. Then, who knows? We could settle there or go somewhere else. If we have money, anything can be accomplished."

Lady Li stood up and paced. Leave Peking? Leave China! The idea had never really seemed a possibility. Could she really leave her homeland? "When would we need to leave?" she asked. "Now?"

"Oh no," he said. "There are boats heading down the canal all the time. And, of course, I couldn't sell your land without your permission. But I have made some contacts, and know what to do to get us out quickly. At least, for now I do. Should war break out, we might have to leave immediately. War changes everything."

"So we don't have to leave now," she said. "But we need to prepare should we have to leave quickly."

"Yes," he said. "The most difficult part will be selling the land. These things don't happen quickly. I have already had the paperwork drawn up, and he assures me he has the money ready. We would need at least a day to sign the papers and have the money exchanged."

"But if war breaks out," Lady Li said, "even a moment

wasted can mean the difference between escape and being trapped." Her breath hitched in her throat. When she fled the Forbidden City with the imperial family, they had time. They spent several days packing all of the empress's gowns and valuables. Anything they couldn't pack, they were able to hide in secret rooms or bury in her garden. But when they fled the Summer Palace days later, there was no warning. Only the imperial family and a few close servants were able to escape in the middle of the night, including her. They left with the clothes on their backs. Most of the servants had to be left behind. Lady Li tried not to dwell on their fate.

Eunuch Bai nodded. "It is a difficult decision, my lady. If we flee too soon, we will forfeit our lives here for the unknown. But if we delay..."

He didn't finish the sentence. He didn't have to. They both knew what could happen if war broke out, or if the Han turned on the Manchu, and they were trapped in Peking. It was a terrifying possibility.

Lady Li swallowed bitterly. "For now, we wait," she decided. "Inspector Gong may have found the girl's killer. Her brother. Give him time to interrogate him. If the brother killed the girl, this will all be over today."

Eunuch Bai couldn't hide his grimace, or his growing dislike for Inspector Gong, as he stood to take the tea tray from the maid who had just returned. "You still put all your faith, your trust, your very safety, in the hands of this man?"

"Who was I supposed to rely on while you were gone?" Lady Li asked. "I appreciate what you have done, but I thought you had abandoned me. I was terrified!"

"I am sorry, my lady..." Eunuch Bai started to say, hanging his head, but Lady Li interrupted him.

"Don't," she said, holding up her hand. "It doesn't

matter. Prince Kung was here as well. He said that he will not abandon us."

"Prince Kung..." Eunuch Bai tried to interject, his irritation growing.

"Is a friend to this family," Lady Li said firmly.

Eunuch Bai sighed and threw up his hands in the air. "I don't know why I bother," he said as he headed for the door. But before he could reach it, the maid returned.

"My lady," she said. "Inspector Gong has returned."

Eunuch Bai grunted. "Everything is just going so well," he said.

Lady Li couldn't help but chuckle. She was glad her friend—because he was not just a servant to her—was back.

"Show him in," she said.

"I'm leaving," Eunuch Bai declared.

"No, you are staying," Lady Li said. "He was concerned for you as well and set his men to searching for your dead body when you didn't tell us where you went. So you stay!"

He crossed his arms and turned his back to the door when Inspector Gong entered.

"Eunuch Bai!" the inspector exclaimed when he walked in. "You are alive."

Eunuch Bai did not reply or turn to face him.

"Eunuch Bai has been very busy making preparations to keep us safe should war come," Lady Li explained. "And we are very glad he is back."

"I see," Inspector Gong said, eyeing the back of Eunuch Bai's head. "Should I know what these preparations are? Is there anything I can do to help?"

"Not at the moment," Lady Li said. "Please tell me you came with good news. Did the brother kill the girl?"

"I don't know," he said, turning to her. "I need your help, one more time."

"Oh?" Lady Li asked, raising an eyebrow.

"The brother says he 'imagines' he killed her when he was in an opium dream, but he doesn't think he really did it," Inspector Gong explained. "But according to the boyfriend, she pawned the family bow and arrow to a foreigner in the legation. If we find out who he sold the bow and arrow to, we might find the killer."

"So you need me to talk to this shop owner?" Lady Li asked. "But the legation is closed to Chinese who don't live there."

"But Concubine Swan got in," he said. "She could tell you how she did it."

"What?" Eunuch Bai asked, whirling around. "Concubine Swan went into the legation?"

"Oh, Concubine Swan has been getting in many places she shouldn't," Inspector Gong said.

Eunuch Bai looked at Lady Li, his jaw agape.

Lady Li held out her hands helplessly. "Everything went wrong without you here."

Eunuch Bai called for the maid, telling her to send Concubine Swan to them. "Well, one thing at a time," he said.

Lady Li felt her cheeks go hot in embarrassment as Concubine Swan entered the room. Her eyes were red-rimmed and her hair scraggly. Her cheek was still red where Lady Li had slapped her. She was not wearing shoes or a nice gown. She nearly collapsed to her knees in front of Lady Li.

"My lady," she cried. "Please don't send me away. I'm so sorry."

"Please," Lady Li said, holding up her hand to silence her. "We...we aren't talking about that right now. We have something else to discuss with you."

"We need to know how you got into the legation on your own," Eunuch Bai said.

Concubine Swan's eyes shot up at him, surprised. "You're back!"

"Yes," he said curtly. "The legation?"

"Oh," she said. "It was quite simple. I was wearing a very simple gown, because I didn't want to look like a lady when I went to the opium house..."

"*What*?" Eunuch Bai nearly shouted.

"Later," Lady Li said, shushing him.

He put his hand to his mouth to keep from yelling and let Concubine Swan continue.

"I think that because I was dressed simply and spoke English, they believed me when I said I worked for Mrs. Gibson," she explained. "For some reason, they didn't recognize me from when I was there before."

"I doubt they take the time to learn our faces," Lady Li said. "I guess we can try it. I can just borrow a dress from my maid."

"Do it now," Inspector Gong said. "I think we are getting close, but we are running out of time."

"I quite agree," Eunuch Bai said, who then slapped his hand back over his mouth, shocked that he would agree with Inspector Gong about anything.

"Are you sure you don't want me to go do whatever it is you need?" Concubine Swan asked. "I've done it before. I am sure I could do it again."

"You have helped quite enough," Lady Li said. "Your methods were reckless, dangerous. To say nothing of the opium den, which we have yet to deal with. I don't want you anywhere near this investigation!" She shook her head. "Go back to your room. I'll deal with you later."

Concubine Swan nodded and backed away out of the room.

Once she was gone, Inspector Gong approached Lady Li and spoke to her in a low voice. "About...what you suggested. Are you still serious about that? I have given it more thought, and I could approach my parents about it. That is, if it would not make you uncomfortable."

Lady Li felt a shiver down her spine as he spoke to her, his voice deep and rippling through her body. She had been serious at the time, and if he was willing to take her, she doubted she would find a better placement for Concubine Swan. But the idea of his lips, his fingers, his body embracing Concubine Swan instead of her filled her with jealousy. But she remembered her earlier resolve, that he needed to be married and out of her life. And she needed to do what was right by Concubine Swan. She pursed her lips, tamped down her feelings, and nodded.

"The offer is still open," she said, her eyes downcast. She could not face him as she said the words.

He hesitated, but then nodded. "Very well. When this is over, I will see what can be done. Shall I wait here while you go to the legation?"

"Certainly," she said as she rushed from the room. She claimed she needed to find her maid and change, but she also needed a moment away from him to collect her reeling thoughts over what she had just done.

18

Inspector Gong chewed his nail nervously as he waited for Lady Li. He eyed Eunuch Bai, but didn't say anything to him. The two both cared for Lady Li in their own ways, and those ways were often at odds with each other. Finally, it was Eunuch Bai who broke the silence.

"So, what of Concubine Swan?" he asked. "Is her reputation ruined?"

"I'm not sure what will happen to her reputation, or that of the household," Inspector Gong said. "But I found her in an opium den down the road."

Eunuch Bai sighed and rubbed his forehead. "That girl's...dissatisfaction with her life has grown by the day. It is only a matter of time before something must be done."

Inspector Gong didn't reply. He didn't know if he would be able to marry the girl himself or not, so he didn't see a reason to get his hopes up.

"She sneaked into the legation as well?" Eunuch Bai asked.

Inspector Gong nodded. "She wanted to help with the

investigation. She knew Lady Li would be furious when she found out she had left the house, so I suppose it was her way of redeeming herself."

"Sorry chance of that happening," Eunuch Bai said, shaking his head. "This is...simply unforgiveable."

"Where does she get her opium on a daily basis?" Inspector Gong asked. "I've seen her in the past, here in the house, with that...opium haze people get. Lady Li knows she eats it here in her home, right?"

"She knows," Eunuch Bai said tightly. "She must get it from her maids. Though where the girls get it, I have no idea. Lady Li has a soft heart, and she feels sorry for Concubine Swan, so she knew the girl was taking it, but she didn't push her to stop."

Inspector Gong grunted to himself. Perhaps he shouldn't take Concubine Swan. His mother would never forgive him for bringing an opium eater into the house. If he did marry her, he would have to forbid her from taking opium. But he had seen many addicts in his line of work. Quitting was not so easy. Just look at Jiaolong. His father disowned him and he still had not quit. What if Concubine Swan could not stop either?

When Lady Li walked back into the room in a simple dark blue robe, he completely forgot about Concubine Swan. Her hair was pinned in a simple bun on top of her head, she wore flat cotton shoes, and she wore no makeup. Yet even in this simple arrangement, attempting to mimic a servant, she looked exquisite. He did not think anyone would believe she was simply a maid. Her elegant bearing was not something that she could simply cast aside.

"You should...umm..." Inspector Gong stammered. "You should cast your eyes downward. A servant would not hold her head high."

"Oh, of course," Lady Li said as she looked down demurely, which had the effect of only making her more alluring.

Inspector Gong blew out a long breath. "Well, it will have to do. Come along."

Together, they climbed into her sedan chair and headed toward the legation.

"You should get out before we get in sight of the legation," Inspector Gong said. "We don't want the guards to see you getting out of a sedan chair."

"Of course," Lady Li said. "What is the name of the shop I am looking for?"

"I'm not sure," he said as he peeked through the windows of the chair. "He only said the man's name was Mr. Big, and he had a shop inside the legation where all the servants would sell goods from their hometowns for money. Much more than they could get at a shop outside the legation."

"I am sure I'll find it," she said. "Oh! I should have brought something to sell him."

"Just pretend you are buying for your master," Inspector Gong suggested. "Bolin said that the foreigners love to buy the items as decorations for their homes."

"How strange," Lady Li said.

Inspector Gong nodded. "Just be as quick as you can. I'll wait for you."

She gave him a small smile and then turned away. They sat in uncomfortable silence for a moment.

"I'd marry you if I could," he finally said, unable to keep the words inside any longer.

"I know," she said, not turning to look at him.

They fell silent again. There was nothing more to say on

the matter. They both wanted what they could not have, so there was no point in dwelling on it.

When they were around the corner from the legation, Inspector Gong leaned out the window and told the chair bearers to stop.

"Be careful," he told Lady Li as she stepped out. "Come back as quickly as you can."

"I will," she said with a small smile and a nod of her head.

He waited a moment, and then got out of the chair himself and peeked around the corner to see what happened. As she approached the gate, he saw her drop her chin to her chest, apparently remembering what he told her about keeping her head down. She walked up to the guards and spoke to them. He started to get nervous when he saw them wave another guard over, but they were only asking him to open the gate. He breathed a sigh of relief once she was inside. But the tension within him grew again the longer she was gone.

He was pacing back and forth nervously when he saw an old man, his head shrouded, walking down the road past the legation. He looked somewhat familiar, but he wasn't sure who it was since he could not see his face. Suddenly, the old man stepped into the street, right into the path of an oncoming horse-drawn carriage. A woman shrieked as the horses whinnied and reared up on their back legs. The man fell backward, so he was not trampled. The owner of the carriage, a white man, jumped out of the carriage to see what had happened. He was followed out of the carriage by his wife and daughters.

Inspector Gong started to run over, but from behind him, he heard countless angry shouts. He looked, and a whole mob of people were marching down the road toward the legation. He felt his heart sink, and he knew who the old man was. The white man was gingerly helping the old man to his feet, checking to see if he was injured. Inspector Gong grabbed the old man by his arm and ripped off the head covering.

"Zhao!" Inspector Gong exclaimed. "What have you done?"

"What you lack the courage to do," he said.

Inspector Gong turned to the white man and his family and told them to get back into their carriage. Of course, he could only do so in Chinese, and the family did not seem to understand, so he did his best to use his arms to herd them inside. They still appeared confused, until they heard, and then saw, the angry mob running toward them. The women screamed as they scrambled to get back inside.

"Get into the legation!" Inspector Gong yelled at their driver, who was Chinese, but it was too late. The guards could not open the gate, admit the carriage, and close it in time. Inspector Gong ran for the guards and pointed toward the family in the carriage, urging them to help him get them inside. Two of the guards went with him, but two more stayed back to protect the gate and call for reinforcements.

Inspector Gong and the guards stood between the white family and the angry crowd. He motioned for the driver of the carriage to follow them, but it was too late. The mob grabbed the driver and dragged him down, kicking and beating him. With no one holding the horses' reins, there was no way to stop them when they finally got spooked enough to run. The horses lurched forward, and then took off at a full gallop through the crowd, trampling dozens of people, but thinning the crowd enough that Inspector Gong and the guards took the opportunity to run for the legation. As they made it to the gate, the door flew open and the family were pulled safely inside. Inspector Gong was shut outside the gate.

"Fire!"

Inspector Gong heard the crack of rifles into the crowd. There were screams and a loud crash as the carriage tipped over. Through the smoke of the rifles, Inspector Gong could not see if anyone had been injured.

"Ready!"

Inspector Gong looked at the guards, and realized they were about to fire again.

"Aim!"

He grabbed the rifle of one of the men next to him. "Stop!" he yelled in English. One of the other reinforcement guards who had arrived, grabbed Inspector Gong, turned him around, and then kneed him in the gut. Inspector Gong fell to his knees.

"Fire!"

Another round of rifle cracks rang out. More screams. More panic. But the crowd did clear. He heard the sound of trumpets as the imperial guard arrived. The guards lowered their rifles. Prince Kung was among the men who had arrived. Inspector Gong got to his feet and went to the prince's side.

"Are you injured?" the prince asked.

"No," he lied. The kick to his gut seemed to have reinjured his ribs, but he would not worry the prince with that.

The prince nodded and went to the guards. He had a heated discussion with them. The chief of British police then came out, and there was more yelling. Inspector Gong looked out at the street. There were at least three dead bodies lying there. Mourners were already wailing over them. More would come, as would more rioters.

More legation guards, dozens of them, arrived. The

foreign police went inside the legation and locked the door. Prince Kung huffed as he walked away.

"What is happening?" Inspector Gong asked.

"The legation is completely shut down," he said. "No one will get in or out until the killer is named and the ports are reopened. The first of the battleships will arrive in two days."

"What does this mean?" Inspector Gong asked. "What are your instructions?"

"You must name your killer by the end of the day tomorrow," the prince said. "Or else I will."

19

"*E*xcuse me," Lady Li said to a young Chinese woman when she entered the legation. "Do you know where Mr. Big's shop is?"

The young woman paused for a moment and looked her up and down. "I haven't seen you here before," she finally said.

"I'm new. I just started at the Gibson house," Lady Li replied, feigning confidence.

"I heard they took on a new maid," she said. She must have been referring to Concubine Swan. Concubine Swan had told people she worked for the Gibsons as well. "You're a brave soul, I must say."

"Why is that?" Lady Li asked, sure the girl was talking about Weilin's murder but wanting her opinion on the matter. Concubine Swan had found out quite a bit by talking to the other maids in the concession.

"That Mr. Gibson," the maid said, shaking her head. "Can't keep his hands to himself, is what I heard. Every maid they have taken on has had to leave eventually."

Lady Li nodded, mulling this over. He must have eventually gotten all of their maids pregnant. Lady Li wondered what Mrs. Gibson thought about it. If she wondered why so many of her maids had left. Didn't she say that Weilin had been there for years? Weilin must have been very lucky, or she had found a way to take care of the pregnancies in the past.

"Maybe he learned his lesson after the death of the last maid," Lady Li said. "He hasn't tried anything with me."

The maid scoffed. "That arrow should have pierced *his* heart. Worst of the worst of the foreign scum. Raping our girls, poisoning our men with opium."

"I hope you don't think poorly of me for working there," Lady Li said.

"We all have to do what we must to survive," the maid said consolingly. "Just be careful if you think you're going to pawn something you pinched. I wouldn't sell it in the legation. Gibson would be sure to find out."

"Oh, I haven't stolen anything," Lady Li said. "Yet." The other maid smiled and Lady Li did likewise. "I just heard Mr. Big bought items from the countryside and wanted to learn more about it."

"Well, if you go down the street and to the left," the maid said, pointing. "You'll see his shop on the right."

"Thank you so kindly," Lady Li said and she turned to leave.

"Hey, what was your name?" the maid called after her, but Lady Li pretended she didn't hear her and picked up her pace.

Mr. Big's shop was quite easy to find. His shop had a large picture window with his name on it in large white and gold letters painted on it: MR. BIG'S GOODS AND SUNDRIES. A little bell rang as she opened the door.

"Just a moment," a voice called from somewhere deep in

the store, but Lady Li couldn't see him over the stacks of items piled everywhere. There were mounds of furniture in various condition, from beautifully carved and polished to dirty and falling apart. There were boxes of clothes and sticks of tea cups. Beautifully embroidered lotus slippers were strewn about, some in pairs but many missing their mates. Porcelain jars and vases, some chipped, some not, sat on shelves, along with cloisonné boxes. Some of the pieces were lovely, but most of it was junk. Lady Li wondered just how much the foreigners were willing to pay for items she would likely just throw away had they been in her home. Except for the household god carvings she saw sitting irreverently in a corner. She couldn't believe someone would sell them, much less that other people would buy them. It was dishonorable. She shook her head.

"Sorry about that," said a kindly voice. "How can I help you?"

Lady Li looked up, and then had to look back down. Standing before her was the shortest, sweetest looking man she had ever seen. He only came up to about her waist. His face looked like he was older, possibly in his forties or even fifties, with pale blonde hair.

"Well, you don't need to gape, darlin'," he said in an accent she had never heard before.

"I'm sorry," she said, shaking herself out of her shock. "I was…just expecting…"

"Someone bigger?" he asked with a laugh and flick of his wrist. "That's why I just love my name. It gets the new customers every time!"

Lady Li let out a relieved laugh, glad she was not the only person to be taken in by the man's joke.

"Come on back and sit a spell," he said as he walked to a display case in the back of the room. He climbed up onto the stool behind it and motioned for Lady Li to sit on a stool by the front. "Can I get you some sweet tea?"

"Sweet tea?" she asked, confused.

"You must try it," he said. "It's the only way we drink it back home."

"Where is home?" Lady Li asked as she sat.

"Atlanta," he said. "Georgia," he continued at the blank look on her face. "America," he finally clarified.

"Of course," Lady Li finally said. Other than California or New York she was hopeless at American geography.

"It's no problem," he said as he poured her a cup of tea and then dropped a whole spoonful of sugar into it. "I'm sure there is no need for you to be very familiar with it."

"I think you must know a lot about China, though," Lady Li said, trying to flatter him. "Since you collect so many...interesting things." She doubted he knew as much as he thought, or lacked respect. He eyed the colorful sacrificial wreath he had for sale behind the table. Such a thing should only be used in a funeral procession and then burned. The fact he was selling one as a decoration made her skin crawl.

He handed her the cup and she held it gingerly in her hand for a moment before sipping it. She nearly chocked when she realized the tea was cold.

"It's supposed to be cold," Mr. Big said, seeing her wide eyes. "That's how we like it. What do you think?"

"It's very...interesting," Lady Li said politely. She had gotten somewhat used to tea with sugar and cream through her visits with the British ladies, but she had never had it served to her cold. She thought it was quite uncouth.

"You're a very well-mannered maid," Mr. Big said, not in an accusatory way, more amused, but Lady Li realized her class was starting to show through her disguise.

"It is new to me," Lady Li said, trying to recover, "but thank you for your hospitality."

"Of course," he said. "Oh, yes. As you said, I love traveling the Chinese countryside, looking for new and interesting things. I've been all the way to Mongolia, to Canton, and out west to Szechuan."

"That is amazing," Lady Li said, considering that other than when she had to flee north to Jehol, she'd never be out of Peking.

"This is an incredible country," he said. "Where are you from?"

She opened her mouth to say Peking, but then remembered to stop herself. "Kwangsi Province," she said.

"Oh! Kwangsi!" he said, slapping his hands to his cheeks in excitement. "So beautiful! The mountains just go on and on and on, don't they? And so green. How do you survive cooped up here in the city?"

"We all do what we must," she said as she took another sip of the vile tea.

"So true," he said as he took a sip of the tea and sighed in contentment. "So what can I do for you?"

"Oh, of course," she said, setting down her cup. "I was actually looking for something to buy. Something for my father. I have to go home for Spring Festival..." She cut herself off, remembering that in one of Weilin's letters she said she would not be allowed to go home for Spring Festival. "I mean, you know we cannot go home for Spring Festival, so I wanted to send my family, my father, a gift instead."

"I see," he said, tapping his chin. "What kind of thing does your father like?"

"Umm...hunting," she said. "Maybe a hunting knife...or bow?"

"How strange," he said, pulling out a notebook. "You know, I had just the thing in here a few days ago."

"Really?" Lady Li asked, leaning forward to look at his book.

He angled the book so she couldn't read it. "Yes, a beautiful hand-carved bow and arrow, from Kwangsi Province, no less. I had considered keeping it for myself."

"What happened to it?" Lady Li asked.

"Some sort of family feud, I suppose," he said. "The girl who sold it to me, her brother came in the next day, demanding it back. Said she had no right to sell it. That is was his birthright. That his uncle gave him the money to buy it back."

"His uncle?" Lady Li asked, raising her eyebrow. This was the first she had heard of an uncle.

"Well, she had sold it to me, you see," he said. "So of course I had to mark the price up to sell it, make my money back and a profit." Lady Li nodded. "I could have gotten a lot more for it in the States. It would have looked just beautiful on a wall, over a mantle place."

"But the brother, he demanded it back?" Lady Li asked, leaning forward expectantly.

"Yes, but he didn't have the money," he said. "I gave him a good price, but he didn't have it at first. So he left. But then he came back a while later with more money, said his uncle gave it to him. So I had to let it go. I thought about telling him it had sold while he was gone. It was that beautiful. But he was so...adamant about getting it back. He grabbed me by the collar. Nearly dragged me over the counter." He closed his eyes and shook his head.

"I'm so sorry," she said.

"Well, it's gone now," he said. "But let me see if I can find something else for you." He hopped down off of the stool and started rummaging around in the shop. "I'm sure I can find something suitable for you."

"You really needn't go to any trouble," she said as she moved toward the door.

"It's no trouble," he said. "I'll just...What's going on out there?"

Lady Li looked out the door while Mr. Big made his way to the large window. There were a dozen soldiers running toward the front gate.

"Oh no!" Lady Li exclaimed. There must be some sort of trouble. She flung the door open and ran out into the street.

"Get back inside!" one of the soldiers yelled as he passed.

She ignored him and ran to the end of the street and peered around the corner at the gate. It was then that she could hear the yells and screams coming from outside. The door in the gate opened and she saw a foreign family stumble through. As the door shut, she heard the crack of rifles.

Lady Li gasped and put her hand to her mouth. What was happening out there? What should she do?

She looked around and saw the legation residents running for their homes and shuttering their businesses. She looked back at Mr. Big's shop and saw him using a long hook to pull a metal screen down over the large window. Then he went inside and locked the door, covering the small window with a blind.

A second round of rifle fire rent the air. She could see dust and smoke rising from the street beyond the legation gate.

Then, all was silent. She saw important-looking men in uniforms and suits head out of the gate door. After a moment, they came back in.

"Get back to your home," one of them barked at her when they passed.

She gave a slight curtsey. "Yes, sir," she said, keeping her eyes down. Once they rounded the corner, she ran for the gate.

"Let me out, please," she said to one of the guards.

"Sorry, miss," the guard said. "No one gets in or out. It's too dangerous right now."

"But...but I must..." she tried to protest.

One of the guards pushed her away rather roughly. "Back to your employer. Now!"

Lady Li walked down the road, back toward Mr. Big's shop. What was she to do now? She needed to let Inspector Gong know what she had discovered. She went to the post office so she could hopefully send him an urgent message, but the post office had been shuttered as well.

She stood there for a moment, unsure of what to do. She didn't have a home or place of employment to go to. She could call on the Gibsons or Lady Highcastle, but she was dressed as a maid! Surely they would question why she was dressed in such a manner.

She chewed her nail nervously. What was she to do now?

20

*L*ady Li paced in front of the post office for a minute, but eventually a regiment of guards came through again, barking at everyone who was loitering or even looking out their windows that they needed to be indoors. She remembered that Mr. Big had a box of clothes for sale in his shop. Maybe she could buy a gown from him that would be somewhat presentable. She went back across the street and knocked on the door.

"Mr. Big?" she called. "Are you still in there?"

He peeked out of the blind and then opened the door just a crack. "I'm so sorry, honey," he said, "but during a lockdown I'm not allowed to have my business open. You should get home."

Lady Li felt a bit of panic rise up in her throat. She looked back to the gate and then back at Mr. Big with pleading eyes, unsure of what to say.

He sighed and took pity on her. "Come inside," he said, opening the door a little wider.

"Thank you!" she gasped as she slipped inside. He shut and locked the door behind her.

"It's no problem," he said. "Us fine folk have to stick together." He gave her a wink.

"What do you mean?" she asked, confused.

"I might not look it," he said as he went back to his stool behind the counter, "but I come from a long line of southern gentlemen. My family has been in the States since they were the Colonies. We have one of the largest plantations in Georgia. I had to leave America to find quality people with money older than mine."

Lady Li pressed her lips as she sat on her stool a little uneasily. She wasn't sure what this strange little man was getting at.

"Come now," he said with a smile as he heated up a new pot of tea. "If you saw someone like you walk into a room would believe her if she said she was a maid?"

Lady Li blushed a little. "Probably not," she admitted. "I have spent my life training to act a certain way. It is a hard habit to break."

"It's not an act," he said with a gleam in his eye. "It's how you are. You were born this way. The question is, why you would don the clothing and guise of a maid, sneak into the legation, and drop by my shop?"

She sighed. She was a terrible investigator. She didn't know why Inspector Gong kept trusting in her to help him.

"The bow and arrow you sold," she finally said. "They were used to kill the maid at the Gibsons' house. I needed to know who bought them."

"Were they really?" he asked, his mouth and eyes wide as he poured a cup of hot water and dropped some Chinese tea leaves into it.

"I'm surprised her manner of death is not common knowledge," Lady Li said. "It was quite shocking."

"The police have been keeping the details close to their

chests," he said as he slid the cup of tea in front of Lady Li. "We all know she was shot, from across the street. But I reckon we all assumed it was a gun shot. I don't know why I didn't think of the bow and arrow I sold."

"It was a very odd way to kill someone," Lady Li said as she held the teacup in her hands, letting it warm her fingers. "But the killing seemed personal. Like the killer was sending a message."

Mr. Big leaned forward on the display case conspiratorially. "So you think the brother killed his sister with the bow and arrow. Like a family feud of some sort."

Lady Li sipped her tea and nodded. "It would seem that way. But now I am trapped here, in the legation! I cannot send a message to the Chinese investigator to let him know what happened. They might execute the wrong man!"

"Oh!" Mr. Big gasped, leaning back. "You mean the boyfriend. The one who was employed by the Belvederes. It was a big display when he was arrested. Everyone thought he must have done it. Poor fellow. What a tragedy."

"Can you help me get a message out of the legation?" Lady Li asked. "The post office is closed and I cannot leave."

Mr. Big sighed. "I'm sorry. I can't force the post office to open. But I am sure they will reopen tomorrow morning."

"What am I to do for tonight?" Lady Li asked. "Where am I to stay?"

He chuckled. "I'm sure it wouldn't do for you to stay with me."

She held out her hands helplessly. "I'm sure it wouldn't look good. I have friends here in the legation. Mrs. Gibson and Lady Highcastle. But they know me for who I am, a lady. I can't go to them dressed as a maid."

"Oh, I'm sure I could find you something to wear," he said, hopping off his stool and going into a back room. He returned a moment later with a blue English-style walking dress. "It is hopelessly out of fashion. I wouldn't be able to get much for it. But it might do just for now."

Lady Li held up the gown and looked at it. It reminded her of the dress she wore the first time she returned to the legation, the one that was also out of date.

"Fortunately, the ladies are used to seeing me wear clothes that are old-fashioned," she said.

"Well, this will be perfect," Mr. Big said. "Let's put it on you and I can pin it to make it look like it fits."

"You are too kind," Lady Li said, clutching the dress to her chest. "How can I ever repay you?"

He leaned in again. "Honey, just be sure to come back and tell me all the naughty details you learn while staying with the Gibsons and we are golden."

Lady Li couldn't help but laugh.

*L*ady Li nervously rang the bell at the Gibsons' home. She self-consciously ran her fingers over a frayed edge of her borrowed gown. She hoped they wouldn't notice just how badly damaged the dress was. It had been sitting in a box in Mr. Big's shop for months, apparently, but it was the only one they found that he could pin tight enough to fit her.

A maid opened the door and her mouth gawped.

"Mrs. Gibson, please," Lady Li said quickly. The maid shut the door. She returned only a moment later, ushering Lady Li inside. She was led to the same parlor as before. As soon as she entered the room, Mrs. Gibson rushed to take her hands.

"Lady Li!" she cried. "How are you? How did you even get in? Did you see the trouble at the gate?"

Mr. Gibson was there as well, a concerned look on his face, though he said nothing.

"I'm am fine," Lady Li said. "Though in a bit of trouble. They have locked the gate. No one can get in or out. I am trapped here."

"Well, how ridiculous is that?" Mrs. Gibson said, looking to her husband. "I can understand only letting residents in or out, but people who don't live here? Absurd! Surely you can do something."

He nodded and headed out of the room. "I will see what I can do."

Mrs. Gibson placed her arm around Lady Li's shoulder and ushered her to one of the plush couches. "I had heard they were not letting non-residents in the legation for several days. How did you get inside in the first place?"

"Oh?" Lady Li asked, feigning innocence. "I didn't realize. I was only coming to call on you and they simply let me in. They must have thought I was a maid or something."

"How dreadful!" Mrs. Gibson said, clicking her tongue. "Well, we will have to talk about the lax security around here, especially in such a dangerous time. Not that I am unhappy to see you, my dear."

"I completely understand," Lady Li replied. "I was inside, still near the gate when I heard the gun shots. It was quite unnerving."

"I am sure it was!" Mrs. Gibson said, patting her hand. "Everyone is rather on edge."

"And have they still not found out who killed your maid?" Lady Li asked. "One tragedy after another."

"Well, I think everyone is certain the young man from across the street did it," Mrs. Gibson said. "It usually is a lovers' quarrel, these sorts of things."

Lady Li nodded sympathetically, wondering just how acquainted Mrs. Gibson was with lovers' quarrels that ended in death.

"Have you been able to find a new maid?" Lady Li asked.

Mrs. Gibson sighed. "No, not yet. I dread having to go through the process again."

"Again?" Lady Li asked.

"Well, Weilin had been with us for some time, but we have had other maids and kitchen staff leave on an almost rotating basis!" she explained. "They never seem to last more than a few months."

"Why do you think that is?" Lady Li asked, though she had a theory of her own.

"Who can tell?" Mrs. Gibson asked. "Work ethic I suppose. We never had this problem retaining staff in England."

Or maybe Mr. Gibson didn't have a habit of forcing himself on his English staff, Lady Li thought to herself bitterly.

They both looked up when they heard the door open. "Well, she's right," Mr. Gibson announce. "They aren't letting anyone in or out. I tried to reason with Chief Barnhart, that the young woman doesn't live here and needed to return to her own family, but he wouldn't hear of it. She's stuck here, it seems."

"I can't even get a letter out?" Lady Li asked. "I went to the post office first thing and they were closed. I would like to let my children know that I am at least safe."

He sat on a chair across from them and shook his head. "I'm afraid not," he said. "They don't want anyone leaving their homes, so that means no businesses can be open either."

"How ridiculous!" his wife exclaimed.

"I know it seems extreme and inconvenient," Mr. Gibson replied. "But it is for everyone's safety. They said they will consider allowing only the most necessary businesses open tomorrow."

"Then I suppose you are stuck here, my dear," Mrs. Gibson said, reaching over and patting Lady Li's hand.

"I am so sorry to be a bother," Lady Li said, genuinely distraught over being unable to get a message to Inspector Gong or her family. With her gone, Concubine Swan would be the mistress of the house. She worried what the girl would do in her absence. At least Popo would be there to mind the children.

"You are no trouble at all!" Mrs. Gibson said, her face lighting up. "You can stay in the guest room. And I am sure I can find something suitable for you to sleep in. And we can have a lovely dinner."

"That sounds wonderful," Lady Li said.

*A*fter an early dinner and drinks by the fireplace, Mrs. Gibson led Lady Li to the guest room. She was able to find an appropriate nightgown among her daughter's things. Once Mrs. Gibson had left, Lady Li inspected the room she was in. The window faced the street and the houses across it. She remembered that Weilin had been killed in a room facing the street. She looked around the room, but did not see anything out of place. Surely they had not put her in the same room where a girl had been killed only days before.

She returned to the window and looked out it. There were some smudges on the glass. She reached up with the sleeve of her gown to wipe them away and noticed that the calking was bright white around some of the panes. They had been newly replaced. She gasped. These must have been the panes that had been shattered by the arrow. This was the room where Weilin had been killed! How grotesque!

Lady Li shook her head and climbed into bed. She shivered, but not from the cold. The girl's murder had not yet been solved. Her body had not yet been laid to rest. Her spirit was most likely still trapped here in this room. No food had been left out. The ghost was probably beyond starving.

"I'm sorry," Lady Li whispered. "We are very close to finding your killer. I promise."

She felt a slight breeze blow through the room and she felt a chill up her spine. She thought at first that Weilin's ghost must be nearby, but then she noticed the door to the room was slowly opening.

"Lady Li?" Mr. Gibson asked, peeking his head into the room. "Are you there?"

Lady Li jumped from the bed and pulled a thin blanket about her. "What do you want?" she asked.

He entered the room with a smile and closed the door. "Forgive me," he said. "I just wanted to make sure you were comfortable. My wife has already gone to bed with a headache so she sent me to check on you."

Lady Li wondered if Mrs. Gibson regularly went to bed with headaches. "I'm fine," she said. "Well, as fine as can be considered what happened in this room."

"I was hoping you wouldn't realize that," he said. "I am sorry, but this is the only unoccupied room in the house at the moment. I hope you are not too uncomfortable."

"I would be more comfortable if you would send a servant up with some warm food," she said. "You need to care for the girl's spirit until she can be sent to the next life. She will be starving."

Mr. Gibson laughed, then he realized she was not laughing with him. "You are serious?"

"I would not joke about sharing a room with a hungry ghost," Lady Li said.

Mr. Gibson rolled his eyes. "You pathetic heathens are all the same. Even someone has high-class as yourself still believes the stupidest things."

"How dare you?" Lady Li said, her eyes burning with fury.

"Stupid," he repeated, but then he licked his lips. "But endlessly beautiful." He stepped closer to her. "Such lithe bodies. Long, silken hair." He reached out as if to touch her but she slapped his hand.

"Do not touch me," she ordered.

He laughed. "You have more spirit than your prede-cessors."

"I am not a servant," she said. "I don't have to accept your advances to keep my job. Get out of my room or I will scream."

"And who will believe you?" he asked. "Servant, concubine, wife. Aren't all you Chinese women the same? Your only purpose is to serve a man. But you don't have a man, do you, Widow Li?"

"I am *Lady* Li," she said. "And you will address me as such."

"I've never been with a Chinese lady before," he said, reaching out and taking a stand of her hair in his hand. "Your men do a good job keeping you hidden. This could be quite a pleasurable experience, for both of us."

She shook her hair free from his hand and moved back again. "You were here that night, weren't you? The night Weilin was killed."

"It was a shocking sight," he said. "We were standing over there, on the other side of the bed. I had ordered her to be here waiting for me while I snuck out of that dreadful play. She had her head down demurely..."

"Think you mean frightened," Lady Li interrupted. "How could she resist you? Her employer? She had a family to support. You took advantage of her..."

He waved her off. "Oh, they all claim that. Yet every one of them ended up in my bed. It's a privilege for them to serve me."

"A privilege?" Lady Li scoffed. "They have all ended up jobless or dead. You ruined their lives!"

"Oh, poppycock!" he blustered. "They are all whores. They can't help it. Every man here will tell you the same story of how easy it is to seduce their maids."

Lady Li couldn't believe what she was hearing. Bolin

had said that all the maids were chaste to protect their jobs, yet most of them were probably having to face down their employers every night. The poor girls. She would need to speak to the mission about it. They were the ones arranging employment for the girls who could speak English. They needed to know about this.

"I am not a servant, nor a whore," Lady Li said. "You will get out of my room, now."

"Come now, Lady Li," he said, rushing up to her and pinning her arms to her side. "Don't you want to know what a proper English cock could do for you? Surely you need it."

"This is your last warning," Lady Li said firmly.

He reached up and grabbed her breast. He groaned, first with pleasure, and then with pain as Lady Li's knee met his groin. He slowly sunk to the floor. Once again, Prince Kung's training had come in useful.

"Get out of my room," Lady Li said. "And have some food brought up for Weilin's ghost, or you will never use that cock again."

"You will pay for this," he grunted as he made his way to his feet, but he remained hunched over. He stumbled to the door and out to the hallway.

Lady Li let out a relieved sigh. She climbed back into her bed even though she knew she wouldn't sleep that night. She felt a warmth envelop her, and she had a feeling Weilin's ghost was pleased.

*M*r. Gibson did not return to Lady Li's room that night.

The next morning, she was surprised to receive a breakfast tray in her room. She thought maybe Mr. Gibson was punishing her, but the maid explained that it was normal for married women to have breakfast in their rooms.

"How odd," Lady Li said.

"My lady," the maid said hesitantly. "I...we...the girls downstairs, we just wanted you to know that we know what you did...to Mr. Gibson."

Lady Li looked up at her. "And...?" she asked, wondering if she was about to get a chastisement from a servant.

"It was brave of you," she said. "We are glad he finally got what he deserved."

"He deserves far worse," Lady Li said.

"We saw him limping down the stairs," she said as she covered her mouth to stifle a giggle. "And he saw us laughing at him."

"I hope I didn't make your lives more difficult," Lady Li said.

"I doubt that could be the case, ma'am," she said. "But don't worry about us. All life is suffering, and this is only temporary."

Lady Li gave the girl a wan smile. She had not relied on her Buddhist teachings for years. She was glad the girls found some comfort in them.

"I only wish I could do more," she said.

The maid waved her off. "I also thought you would like to know that the post office is open. I don't think they are opening the gates yet, but you can at least send a message to your daughters."

Lady Li nearly jumped out of bed. "Help me dress," she said.

21

*I*nspector Gong was out of time. He had one day to name the killer. Even though he had two strong suspects—the boyfriend and the brother—he couldn't be certain of either one. He felt like he was missing something. He was hesitant to act without whatever information Lady Li had gained from inside the legation, but he had no idea when he would hear from her again. The post office was closed, but no one could even get a message to him since no one was allowed out.

He would have to solve this case on his own.

He went back to the Ministry of Justice to interrogate the brother one more time. He would either get a confession out of him or the brother would name the real killer.

When he opened the door to the cell, he was shocked at the state the brother was in. He was still groggy and his eyes glazed over as though he was still under the effects of the opium. He was shaking to the point of convulsing.

"What's wrong with him?" he asked the guard.

"When we lock up opium eaters, they often act this way when they can't have their opium," the guard said. "But this..." He shook his head. "This is the worst I have seen. I think the opium destroyed his brain."

Inspector Gong shut the door and dragged Jiaolong to a sitting position. "Sit up," he ordered. The boy sat as best he could, but it was like his body was noodles as he slumped over.

"How long have you been eating opium?" Inspector Gong asked.

"How many grains of sand are in the sea?" the boy asked.

Inspector Gong slapped the boy across the face. "Wake up and answer me," he said.

Jiaolong opened his eyes and did his best to sit up, but it clearly took a lot of effort.

"You said you dreamed of killing your sister," he said. "Tell me your dream. What did you see?"

Jiaolong looked at his hands. "I hide the bow and arrow in the leg of my pants. The clothes, I stole them, but I don't remember from who. I walk up to the legation, they just let me in. They think I'm a goddamn running dog."

"Running dog" was what people called Chinese who wanted to be like the foreigners. It was usually reserved for Chinese Christians, but anyone who did the bidding of a foreigner could be called a running dog.

Inspector Gong nodded. He remembered that even on tightened security, the guards simply admitted Lady Li to the legation when they thought she was a maid. So far, his story made perfect sense.

"I go to the house where I know my sister is living. It is dark, but I know she is there. I look down the street and I see him, the man she lets touch her, coming toward me. I look at the house across the street. I open my arms and I fly to the roof."

Inspector Gong tried not to groan as he sighed. Jiaolong probably didn't remember how he made it to the roof so his mind was filling in the blanks. He just nodded for the boy to continue.

"There is a light on in one room," he says. "She is looking out the window. She is crying. I see him enter the house. I raise my bow. I want to kill him. I'm supposed to kill him. He is the opium king."

"What do you mean you are supposed to kill him?" Inspector Gong asked. "Did someone order you to do it?"

"I only have one arrow," the boy continues as if he didn't hear the question. "So I wait. She moves away from the window when he enters the room. He approaches her. She steps back. He puts his hands on her. He kisses her. Damn bitch. She let him do it! She pulls away from him and stands by the window. I let my arrow fly."

Inspector Gong rubs his head, sickened over what he is hearing. The girl was crying, trying to get away from Mr. Gibson. He thought about what Lady Li said about the girl not having a choice but to give into him. Even her own brother saw her as the person at fault when she clearly was trying to escape. No wonder she didn't try to report him or get help. Who would have believed her?

"So you killed her," Inspector Gong said through gritted teeth, trying his best not to beat the boy to death right now.

"I flew down from the roof," the boy said, continuing his story. "I went back to my uncle. I gave him the bow as a gift. He told me I was a good son. I sleep. I am at peace."

"What?" Inspector Gong asked. "Your uncle?" This was the second time the uncle had come up. Could he have played a larger role in this?

"My father disowned me," Jiaolong said. "But my uncle,

he said he would adopt me. He knows the true meaning of family."

"In exchange for what?" the inspector asked. "He said he would adopt you in exchange for what?"

"What?" Jiaolong asked, looking up confused, as if he had forgotten the inspector was there.

"Your uncle?" Inspector Gong asked, grabbing Jialong by the collar. "Did he tell you to kill Weilin?"

"I...I don't remember," he said. "He...he told me he was proud of me."

"Where is he?" Inspector Gong asked. "Where is your uncle?"

"I don't know," Jiaolong said, his head flopping over again. "He...he came to me. In a dream..."

Inspector Gong balled up his fist and punched the boy in the face. He didn't punch him hard, but in his state, it was enough to knock him out. Idiot that he is, he practically admitted to the killing. His "dream" was surely enough of a confession. He had to have done it.

But Inspector Gong knew there was more going on. He needed to find this uncle. Find out his role in Weilin's death. He went outside and found a few of his men.

"We need to find the boy's uncle," he said. "He is a Zhao. He would have been seen with Jiaolong. Check every opium house in the city until you find him."

"Yes, sir," they said as they ran off.

He decided to go home to grab a bite to eat and wait for news. If the men didn't find Zhao before the deadline, he would charge Jiaolong. It would be an unsatisfactory solution, but he could just add it to the list of other cases that kept him up at night.

But when he got home, his mother immediately approached him and he lost his appetite.

"Not now," he said. "I can't be bothered with marriage talk."

"You hate me so much?" she asked. "You give me an impossible task and then refuse to discuss it with me when I have not seen you in days?"

"Surely there is one girl in this entire country you can find who meets my perfectly reasonable requests," he said, exasperated. "Can't you just take care of this without bothering me?"

"I cannot!" she said. "I cannot find a girl. I have asked every family, every matchmaker, every fortuneteller! Please, let me find you a bound-foot girl. It is only proper."

He sighed and shook his head. He hadn't wanted to discuss this now, and he was probably making a mistake, but what else was new?

"I found a girl I will accept," he finally said. "The question is if you will accept her."

His mother nearly fell into the chair next to him. "You found a girl? On your own? Who you will accept? Yes! Tell me! I will call on her parents tomorrow."

"You won't talk to her parents," he said. "Not yet. You will have to talk to her mistress. She is a second wife, a concubine, but her husband is dead. Her mistress wants to find her a good new home."

"A woman already married?" his mother asked, frowning. "Very bad luck. She should remain chaste. Honor her husband in death until her own."

"He has his first wife for that," he said. "This girl is still young. Barely twenty, I think. She deserves to be married again."

His mother slowly nodded, considering the implications. "She has flat feet?" she asked. "You said a flat-footed girl. She must not be from a good family."

"She is from a very good family," he said. "She is Manchu."

His mother gasped and put her hands to her cheeks. "A Manchu? Have you lost your senses? This is not that woman, that lady we spoke of before?"

"No," he said, shaking his head. "That woman is the first wife. She is the mistress of the girl I want to marry. You met her the other day. Concubine Swan. She was here looking for me."

"That strange girl? The one who wandered the street alone?" his mother lamented. "You cannot marry a Manchu. It is not legal."

"She is only a concubine," he said. "And I am a fourth son. Who will care?"

"You are friends with the royal family," she said. "Will they not object? Will it hurt your career?"

Inspector Gong nodded. She could have a point. But it could also play in his favor. "I could try to get official permission from the prince," he said.

His mother nodded. "If you do, I will get this girl for you."

"It is agreed then," Inspector Gong said, holding out his hand as if to shake hers. Marriage really was little more than a business transaction.

She slapped his hand away and laughed as she rose to leave. He doubted she would get any sleep either. She would spend the next few days making arrangements for the meeting with Lady Li and for the wedding. Even though the two families had not even discussed the marriage yet, it was practically a done deal—as long as he could get the prince to agree, and he saw no reason why he wouldn't. Unless he failed to name a killer and China ended up at war with the foreign powers. It was tempting. Starting a war to prevent a marriage. It could be worth it.

*T*he next morning, Inspector Gong woke up to an urgent telegram from Lady Li. It said that Jiao-long had purchased the bow and arrow back from Mr. Big. His chest felt heavy. This was the final bit of evidence he would need to charge the boy. He owned the murder weapon just before she was killed. It was enough for a quick conviction. But the note also said something else interesting. She said that Mr. Big said that the boy purchased the bow and arrow as a gift for his uncle.

He threw on his clothes and went to see if his men had found the uncle. He had to be involved. He had come up in every part of the investigation. Maybe he actually killed the girl but convinced the boy he had done it.

"We found him, boss," one of the men said. "He wasn't even trying to hide."

"Did you detain him?" he asked.

"He is waiting for you at the den," the man said. "He said he wouldn't go with us if we weren't charging him with a crime."

"That's fine," Inspector Gong said, but he was a little concerned. Usually people would submit to his men out of fear. This man had no fear and knew the law. He was going to be trouble.

When he arrived at the opium den, he was led to a private room in the back. The man, Zhao Daquan, was sitting serenely, drinking a cup of tea. A beautifully ornate carved bow sat on the table in front of him.

"You realize I have caught you with the murder weapon," Inspector Gong said as he sat down across from him.

"What? This?" Daquan asked, motioning toward the bow. "It belongs to my nephew. He had given it to a host at an opium den to cover his debt. I bought it back from him."

Inspector Gong nodded. He hadn't thought to ask the host at the opium den where he found Jiaolong if he had any of the boy's possessions.

"But I must congratulate you," Daquan went on. "I never thought you would link me to the crime. You did well."

"Aren't you worried I will have you arrested?" Inspector Gong asked.

Daquan shook his head. "You don't have any evidence of my involvement. I didn't kill the girl. I just gave her brother a nudge...and a lot of opium."

"But why?" Inspector Gong asked. "Your own niece? Your own nephew? Does family mean nothing to you?"

"Do you know what is more important than family?" Daquan asked. Inspector Gong shook his head. "Land. You might not think so, living here in a city, but where I come from, a man's family, his soul, his future, his past. It is all in the land. My ancestors, for a hundred generations, were buried on the hill overlooking a stream and all the land for hundreds of li my family owned. They are still there now. But they are looking over another family now. Dozens of families after they split the land like a ripe melon to scoop out its insides."

"Your brother told me he sold the land and came to the city for a better life after decades of war in Kwangsi," Inspector Gong said.

"A better life?" the brother scoffed. "In this stinking cesspool of a city. My brother lives in a hovel. A running dog of the foreign missionaries. He would have starved without their help. He practically sold Weilin to them, promising she would do their bidding. Then she sold herself to that Opium King. When Jiaolong told me she had fallen with child, I knew what I had to do."

"So you had Jiaolong kill her," Inspector Gong said. "To get revenge on your brother for letting go of the family land?"

"It was too easy," he said. "When a person is dreaming opium dreams, they will do anything you ask of them."

"You know Jiaolong, your own blood, he will die for this, for you," Inspector Gong asked, fuming. His hands nearly shaking with rage. "His head will roll."

Daquan calmly sipped his tea. "It is better than my brother deserves," he said. "I would have preferred for his head to roll, but I could not find a way to convince him to kill the girl. He had too much affection, too much pride in her."

"She was a good girl," Inspector Gong said. "She didn't deserve this."

"She was a whore..." Daquan started to say.

"She was a victim," Inspector Gong interrupted. "She hated Gibson. She tried to get away, but Jialong shot her instead of him. If he was going to lose his head for murder he should have killed that bastard."

"I agree!" Daquan said, slapping the table enthusiastically. "I'm glad you see things this way. You are a smart man."

Inspector Gong stood up, grabbed Daquan by the collar, and flung him against the wall. "I am nothing like you!" he yelled. "You ruined your family for nothing. Gibson won't pay for his crimes against that girl or the Chinese people. The only people who will die are two innocent children all for some petty squabble with your brother. You make me sick!"

Daquan only laughed. "I have heard of you, Inspector Gong, running dog for the Manchu prince." He laughed again. "The time of the foreigners, including the Manchu, will come to an end. And all traitors, like you, will go down with them."

"That sounds like seditious talk," Inspector Gong said, lowering Dequan to the floor. "Hey, get in here!" he called to his men who were waiting outside.

"Yes, boss?" the men asked.

"I'm sure you heard this man speaking against the emperor and imperial family," he said to them.

"Sure, boss," they said even though they probably hadn't heard a thing. But Inspector Gong knew he could count on them to support his claims.

"I said no such thing!" Daquan said, growing nervous for the first time.

"I might not be able to have you executed," Inspector Gong said. "But I can have you locked up and beaten for a few days." He turned to his men. "Take him away, charges of sedition."

"No!" Daquan yelled as he was dragged out. "I did no such thing! You'll pay for this, Inspector Gong!"

"You aren't the first enemy I've made in this line of work," Inspector Gong said. "And you won't be the last.

22

*L*ater that day, Inspector Gong called on Lady Li. After the maid admitted him to her office, she nodded for the girl to shut the door. He didn't know what he thought would happen, but he walked to her and held her in his arms. After the day he had, he just needed to feel the comfort of her warmth. What he wouldn't give to be able to come home to such comfort every day. If he could, maybe he wouldn't need baijiu to help him fall asleep every night.

"I heard that Jiaolong was charged with the murder," she said.

He sighed and reluctantly let her slip from his arms. "Yes," he said. "And I had Bolin released. The uncle is being held on suspicion of sedition, but the charges won't hold. He will be released soon."

They went and sat down together on a wooden couch but they continued to hold hands.

"Did the uncle actually kill the girl?" Lady Li asked. "What happened?"

Inspector Gong shook his head. "The uncle wanted

revenge against his brother for losing the family land. And he thought the girl had further dishonored the family by getting pregnant. He gave the boy such a large amount of opium, he couldn't tell fantasy from reality. Even now, days later, the boy's brain is completely muddled. He doesn't know what is happening. When I told him he would be executed for his sister's murder, he didn't even know what I was talking about. He had forgotten about the dream he had told me." He sighed, feeling like a complete failure even though he had solved the crime. "At least he will not suffer when he is executed. His mind is completely gone."

"His poor parents," Lady Li said. "They must be devastated."

"They are," he said. "But I do not think they will cause any more trouble. Prince Kung promised them new land and a new house back in Kwangsi Province if they agree not to incite any more riots. They have agreed. They just want to get away from this place, filled with so many bad memories."

"I don't blame them," Lady Li said, rubbing Inspector Gong's arm. "So the threat of war, it is over?"

"It is," Inspector Gong said. "The ports have reopened and the ships have started to depart. They have already gotten messages to the warships that were on their way and they have agreed to turn away."

Lady Li placed her hand to her heart, no doubt greatly relieved. "That is good to hear. Eunuch Bai, he had made arrangements for us to flee Peking if we had not found the killer in time."

"So that is what he was doing while he was gone?" Inspector Gong asked.

"Yes," Lady Li said, her eyes glancing at the place in the wall where Eunuch Bai's spyhole was. "He knew I would not give him permission to make such plans, so he took it upon himself."

"While I do not agree with his methods," Inspector Gong said, "I cannot fault him for looking out for you."

"Indeed," she said.

They sat in silence for a moment, just enjoying being together and the touch of their hands.

"Lady Li..." he finally started to say, leaning forward, but she let go of his hand, stood, and walked to a table across the room.

"I received a letter," she said, pulling a piece of paper from a drawer. "From your mother. She wishes to call upon me at my earliest convenience to discuss marriage arrangements between her son and the girl named Swan."

Inspector Gong walked over to her and cleared his throat. "Yes, well...you did say the offer was still open."

She nodded as she looked back down at the letter. "I did," she said softly.

He reached over and lifted her chin. Her eyes were wet with tears. "You don't have to reply," he said.

"But I do," Lady Li said as a tear escaped and slid down the left side of her face. "I do."

He took her face in his hands and placed his lips on hers. She put her hands around his neck and held him tight, kissing him back passionately.

"I love you, my lady," he said. "I'll never love Swan the way I love you."

"I know," she said with a nod, pulling away slightly. "But it is what we have to do. You need to speak with the prince, get imperial permission to marry Swan. Then I will speak with your parents."

"I will," he said as he let her slip from his grasp. "He is

very busy trying to smooth things over with the foreigners, but I will speak with him soon."

"That is good," she said with a nod of finality as she wiped the tears from her face. "Good. It is for the best. I am sure Swan will make you happy. I know my husband was pleased with her."

"I am sure she will give me no cause for complaint," he said. "Other than the fact that she is not you."

"Don't hold it against her," Lady Li said. "She has been through so much. Please do good by her."

"I will do my best to be a good husband," he said.

"Then...then I suppose we shall next meet on your wedding day," she said.

Inspector Gong hesitated, but there was nothing left to say. He gave her a slight nod and walked out of Lady Li's office, the taste of her kiss still on his lips.

Lady Li and Inspector Gong will return. Subscribe to my mailing list so you will be the first to find out when it is released!

http://www.twoamericansinchina.com/subscribe

ABOUT THE AUTHOR

 Amanda Roberts is a writer and editor who has been living in China since 2010. Amanda has an MA in English from the University of Central Missouri. She has been published in magazines, newspapers, and anthologies around the world and she regularly contributes to numerous blogs.

Website: http://www.twoamericansinchina.com
Newsletter:
http://www.twoamericansinchina.com/subscribe
Facebook:https://www.facebook.com/TwoAmericansinChina/
Twitter: https://twitter.com/2americanschina
InstaGram: https://www.instagram.com/shreddedpotatoart/
Pintrest: https://www.pinterest.com/amandachina/crazy-dumplings/
Goodreads: https://www.goodreads.com/Amanda_Roberts
Amazon: http://amzn.to/2s9QzAG
BookBub: https://www.bookbub.com/authors/amanda-roberts-2bfe99dd-ea16-4614-a696-84116326dcd1
Email: twoamericansinchina@gmail.com

ABOUT THE PUBLISHER

*VISIT OUR WEBSITE
TO SEE ALL OF OUR HIGH QUALITY BOOKS:*

http://www.redempresspublishing.com

*Quality trade paperbacks, downloads, audio books, and books
in foreign languages in genres such as historical, romance,
mystery, and fantasy.*